D0966667

CRASHING in *Love*

CHARLESTON COUNTY LIBRARY

CRASHING
in *Love*

JENNIFER RICHARD JACOBSON

CANDLEWICK PRESS

This is a work of fiction. All characters, events, and song lyrics appearing in the book are fictional; any resemblance to real people, events, or lyrics is coincidental and not intended by the author.

Copyright © 2021 by Jennifer Richard Jacobson

All rights reserved. No part of this book may be reproduced, transmitted, or stored in an information retrieval system in any form or by any means, graphic, electronic, or mechanical, including photocopying, taping, and recording, without prior written permission from the publisher.

First edition 2021

Library of Congress Catalog Card Number pending
ISBN 978-1-5362-1153-5

21 22 23 24 25 26 LBM 10 9 8 7 6 5 4 3 2 1

Printed in Melrose Park, IL, USA

This book was typeset in Sabon.

Candlewick Press
99 Dover Street
Somerville, Massachusetts 02144

www.candlewick.com

For Jim Talpey, whose story inspired this one

Chapter 1

I skitter around the bedroom I share with my sister Calla, tucking my nightshirt beneath my pillow, picking up the stuffed animals that fell off my bed in the night.

There. My side of the room: neat as a boat galley. Calla's side: hurricane aftermath.

"The world won't come to an end if you leave your bed unmade for one day, Peyton," my oldest sister, Bronwyn, reassures me as she floats back to her own bedroom. She's sweet in the morning, like the maple syrup in her tea.

Bronwyn's probably right. And if I don't hurry, I'm going to miss my chance to say goodbye to my best friend before she leaves for the summer. But one of the gazillion quotes I have pinned on the wall behind my bed reads *Tidy Room, Tidy Mind*, and it's so true. My ten-minute pickup makes me feel as if I'm solidly on the path to creating a better me.

I grab the going-away card I made for Mari, my water bottle (*Motivate, Hydrate, Feel Great*), and my charged phone. "Heading out," I call to my sisters, who are not technically babysitting but are "in charge."

"When will you be back?" Calla asks from the corner of the living room. She's plucking out a new song—"Prickly Thorn, but Sweetly Worn"—on her mandolin.

"I don't know," I say, pushing my glasses farther up my nose. "Soon-ish."

She either doesn't hear me or doesn't really care. It irks me that she even gets to ask. I don't mind if Bronwyn is in charge—she's sixteen. But Calla is thirteen and only eleven months older than I am.

Then I hear an Eleanor Roosevelt quote in my head: "You can often change your circumstances by changing your attitude."

I make an attempt. "Bye, Calla!" I say as cheerily as I can.

Outside, I clip on my bike helmet, tighten the strap, and take off. Early morning is one of my favorite times of day to ride. The country road that winds around Mussel Cove (our tiny town in midcoast Maine) is extremely narrow and has no bike lane. It's also filled with potholes. But at this hour, the early workers (or "the salt," as Mom calls them)—lobstermen, bakers, housekeepers, and news reporters (or should I say news reporter? Mom is the only one in town, and she gets up early to dig for stories at Day's Donuts)—have left, and the late workers ("the pepper")—bartenders, musicians, and chefs—are still snoozing. Which means I can ride closer to the middle of the road, where the pavement is less cracked, swerving around dips and roadkill as needed.

High tide, I notice as I catch my first glimpse of the sun-speckled harbor between the trees. Seagulls are screeching in the distance, which probably means that a fishing boat just returned. Maybe it's Mari's father's boat. Maybe he went out extra early to get back in time to take Mari to her aunt's house in Gloucester.

Gloucester. At first, I was furious with Mari for her last-minute decision to spend the summer helping her aunt (who admittedly just had the cutest baby ever) by looking after her toddler cousins. We had planned our perfect summer—a plan that felt like a promise. This was going to be our summer of working at the Anchorage Hotel (folding towels, setting up beach chairs, filling water pitchers), designing our seventh-grade wardrobe, and finding our first summer boyfriends! I'd even talked Mari into creating a boyfriend list—the top ten musts for the perfect guy—just like mine.

I stand on my bike pedals and pump faster.

Friends should be loyal.

Friends should stick to their plans.

Friends should not break promises.

But then I think of the quote I framed in dried flowers before hanging it above my bed—"The only way to have a friend is to be one"—and I know in my heart that Mari needs to help her family.

We'll just have to share plans and encouragement by phone. "When life gives you lemons—"

Ack! I nearly run over a pair of sunglasses. I quickly pull to the left and—

Omigod! What the—?

There's a pile of clothes in the road. I swerve again and barely avoid it, but my tires hit the gravel, and my bike spins out from under me. As it falls, I try to leap out of the way, but the bike lands on my ankle, and the pedal gouges me. *Ouch!* I hop in circles. My ankle stings outrageously where my skin has been scraped off.

What kind of jerk leaves clothes in the middle of the road, where cars—or bikes—might have to swerve dangerously to avoid hitting them?

I pull my bike off to the side and decide to do the same with the pile so it doesn't cause an accident. *Make that* another *accident*, I think as I hobble over.

I grab the sunglasses and pop them in my pocket. Then I approach the rest of the debris.

I can see what looks like a windbreaker.

Not just a windbreaker.

A hand!

Omigod! *A hand!*

This isn't a pile of clothes. It's a person!

I scream and race back to my bike. Practically choking, I pull up on the handlebars, wanting to get as far from this spot as possible, but—

I drop my bike again.

Buck up, I tell myself. *You are braver than you think*, I tell myself. I pull out my phone and dial 911, then take a deep breath and go back to the body.

It's a boy, I see now, around my age. He's curled up as if he's sleeping, one arm covering part of his face. There's blood on his head, but I don't see any on the road. I stare at his back, hoping to see it rise and fall with his breathing. *Please be alive, please be alive, please be alive!*

As my phone rings, I crouch. "Can you hear me?" I say softly, suddenly afraid of startling him.

He doesn't respond.

"Nine-one-one. What's your emergency?" says a woman

My voice catches. "There's a boy in the middle of

the road. I think he might have been hit by a car. He's not moving. I don't know if he's—"

"What's your name and location?" She sounds calm and helpful.

"Peyton Campbell. I'm in Mussel Cove, on Winding Lane." I look around for a landmark and see a mailbox. "Near 118 Winding Lane."

"Hi, Peyton, honey. This is Mrs. Dwyer. Do you know the boy?"

My first-grade teacher! I didn't know she was a 911 dispatcher now. "No," I squeak. "No—at least, I don't think so. He's curled up on his side, and his arm is covering most of his face. I don't want to move him in case—"

"That's right, Peyton. You don't want to move him. I've got help coming. How old would you say he is?"

I glance down again. "Twelve or thirteen?"

I squat down again and touch his hand.

His fingers twitch.

Omigod! He's alive!

"He's alive!" I shout into the phone.

"Is he conscious?" Mrs. Dwyer asks.

"Can you hear me?" I say to the boy, louder this time. No response.

I stare at the hand that moved, which—and I know this is incredibly strange to say—is nearly perfect in shape. His fingernails are square, and he has a scratch on his thumb.

I reach out and gently take his hand, and I swear on my life I feel movement. "I'm here," I say. "I'm not going to leave you. I promise. Just hang on."

That's when I hear a vehicle coming from the direction of my house. What if the driver doesn't see us in time?

I jump up, wave my arms, and scream, "STOP!"

The driver sees us just as she comes barreling over a small knoll and veers off the road, nearly hitting a tree.

It's Cecelia Hobbs, my neighbor, in her red pickup. She gets out and starts to approach us, but then, realizing, I suppose, that someone else could do exactly what she nearly did—run over this boy again—she gets back in her truck and parks it across the road so no vehicles can pass.

I remember Mrs. Dwyer. "Hello?" She's still on the line. "Mrs. Hobbs is here," I tell her.

"Okay, honey," Mrs. Dwyer says. "I'm going to hang up now. Tell Cecelia that an ambulance is on the way and that she should leave the boy exactly where he is."

The ambulance and a police car arrive just as I finish telling Cecelia what happened.

"He moved!" I tell the EMTs as they lift him into the ambulance on a stretcher. "He moved!"

A police officer asks me to join her on the side of the road. Cecelia follows. I tell the story one more time while the officer takes notes. Then she tells me that she is going to check me for shock, which I think is silly, since I'm obviously in shock. I found an unconscious boy in the middle of the road.

She looks at my hands and touches my forehead. "Are you sweating? Cold?"

I shake my head.

Then she takes a look at my ankle. "It's a nasty cut, but no swelling—and you can stand on it. It will heal on its own. Where do you live? Is anyone there?"

I point in the direction of my house and tell the officer that my older sisters are home.

"I'll get her there," says Cecelia. "We're neighbors."

The sirens begin to whine, and we step farther off the road as the ambulance turns and takes off in the direction of the hospital.

Cecelia retrieves my bike and lifts it into the back of her truck. (She doesn't seem to care that she's still blocking cars in both directions.) I hoist myself up into the passenger seat.

"I wonder who he is," I say as she starts the engine.

"Gray Olsen," Cecelia says.

I stare at her. How does she know that?

"I heard an EMT read it off his student ID. Probably a camper from Brentwood." Brentwood is a summer camp situated in the woods at the end of our road.

I wrap my arms around myself. "I wonder who hit him. And why he was walking into town so early—and alone."

"Let's hope he's able to tell us."

"You don't think he'll wake—that he'll live?" My heart hurts the way it does when I hear a gunshot and know that in all likelihood, a deer has fallen. Or the way it did when Mom told us that Grandpa had died. It's an intense feeling of sadness mixed with something deeper—the knowledge that in seconds, a breathing, spirited life can disappear forever.

"I don't know," she says. "But you certainly did your part, Peyton. You gave him a chance."

Chapter 2

"What happened to your ankle?" Bronwyn asks as I limp into the kitchen.

Calla holds her butter knife in midair. "Yikes! Are you okay?"

I burst into tears. Moments ago, I felt so grown up and capable—calling 911, telling the EMTs and then the police officer what happened—but suddenly I'm the little sister who can hardly say a word through my sobs.

Bronwyn leads me to the couch, and Calla follows. They sit down on either side of me, and Bronwyn says, just like people do in movies, "Take a deep breath and start from the beginning."

And I do. I tell them about the windbreaker, the boy's—Gray's—bloody body, the movement of his hand. How if I hadn't been standing there, Cecelia would have run over him again. I even show them the sunglasses.

"How long do you think he'd been there?" Calla asks.

"The EMTs think it happened about half an hour before I got there, so around seven." I think of him lying there alone. Did he see the car coming at him? Was he conscious for a time? Did he wonder if he would die?

"Mom must have just missed him," Calla says.

Bronwyn agrees. "It's lucky that no other cars came along."

"Or if they did, they veered around him, thinking he was a pile of clothes, like I did."

My sisters nod. Their attention feels like a cozy blanket.

"Do they think he'll live?" Calla asks.

"I don't know," I say. "The police officer—"

"Officer Means?" Bronwyn interrupts. That's the officer on duty at her high school.

"No, it was a woman."

"Officer Dorian," says Calla. "Mom wrote about her last year."

I think for a moment, but I can't recall the article. I feel a familiar pang of guilt for not reading everything Mom writes and vow to try harder. "Anyway, Officer Dorian didn't say one way or the other."

"Mom will have all the details when she comes home," Calla says, and starts to get up.

My mind races to recall more of the specifics, as a way to keep the three of us huddled on this couch for just a moment or two longer. But then my phone rings, and Mom's face appears on the screen.

"Are you all right?" she asks.

"Did they say my name on the police scanner?" I ask. Whereas most mothers are glued to their phones, mine is glued to a police scanner that's on 24/7. She listens for any newsworthy event and tries to place herself and her camera at the scene. I get up from the couch and immediately recall how sore my ankle is.

"No. Officer Dorian called me."

"The officer you did a story on last year," I say, easing off my sneakers and trying to walk the pain out.

"Why, yes! She called me—what a horrible thing! You must be pretty shaken up. I'm on my way home now."

"Is Gray conscious? Will he be okay?"

"The hospital told me"—which really means the nurses who are my mother's sources told her—"that he's in a coma. He's breathing on his own, which is a good sign, but there's no telling when—or if—he'll wake up."

My chest gets that gunshot-in-the-woods feeling again, and I push aside the *if*. He *will* wake up. I know it.

Mom fills me in on what else she knows—he is, in fact, a camper from Brentwood, and his family lives in Connecticut and are on their way—and by the time she hangs up, she's in the driveway. That's how small Mussel Cove is.

It doesn't take long for Mom to decide that I'm fine (though my ankle will probably bruise) and get back to trying to reach the director of Brentwood Camp so she can determine why Gray Olsen was walking along our road in the early hours of the morning. Bronwyn says that Mom's bursts of sympathy are similar to her photography. For a brief moment, she's got you in her lens. You smile, and then *click!* She's off.

It's only then that I realize Mari has texted me no fewer than five times. She is angry with me for not saying goodbye, of course, but wait till she hears why! I sit cross-legged on my bed and, in between apologies, retell the story one more time over text.

"Look him up on Instagram!" she texts, and I do.

His account is private, but sure enough, there's a picture. I adjust my glasses and lean in. He's got blond wavy hair about three shades lighter than mine, a smallish nose, and a sweet smile.

> Mari: Cute!!! Could be your summer boyfriend
>
> Me: OMG Mari! Don't be shallow.
>
> Mari: ☺ You rescued him! He could be your DESTINY
>
> Me: ☺🖤!!

Here's one thing you can say about my best friend: she loves drama. When Bronwyn was in *Romeo and*

Juliet this past spring, Mari insisted that we attend every single performance, even the matinees. And I guess I liked the romance, too, 'cause I gave up my weekend with Dad and Grana on the farm to see it over and over.

I slide off my bed and open the top drawer of my desk, where I keep my precious artifacts. The program from *Romeo and Juliet* is on top. The names of the star-crossed lovers—I just love that expression—are in bold:

ROMEO: FINN WIGGINS
JULIET: BRONWYN CAMPBELL

Finn and Bronwyn had been dating since the Mussel Cove Festival, and everyone said they were perfect for the parts. And they were—right down to the part about being star-crossed.

Inside the program is my boyfriend list. I wrote it right after Finn broke up with Bronwyn. She spent days and days crying in her room. On the rare occasion that she emerged to eat a meal or to share her concerns with Mom ("endless relationship analysis," Calla called it), I looked for the right time to remind Bronwyn that she often criticized Finn—he was a big flirt, he never listened to her, and his sense of humor was cruel—and that she might be better off without him. In fact, why wasn't *she* the one to break up with *him*?

Once, when Bronwyn was cutting her cherry tomatoes into quarters and nibbling on one quarter at a time, she said forlornly, "Finn loves summer tomatoes."

"I thought you said Finn hates vegetables," I reminded her. "That if it doesn't swim, run, or fly, he doesn't eat it."

"Tomatoes are fruits, not vegetables," Calla said.

"I know that," I said. "Everyone knows that. But they don't swim, run, or fly, do they? And Bronwyn doesn't eat anything that moves under its own power, so why would she want to be with someone who is so different from her?"

Bronwyn choked on her almond milk. "That's what he said." Tears rolled down her face again. (Or maybe they had never really stopped.)

Mom shot me a *you're not helping* look.

But I was trying. And I didn't get it. Why do people like Mom and Dad and Bronwyn choose to be with someone who thought and acted so differently from them? Wouldn't my sister be far better off with someone who ignored other girls, listened attentively, told jokes that were actually funny, and didn't eat meat? Kids from four towns go to Mussel Cove High School. How hard could it be to find *that* boyfriend?

I tried again: "You should—"

Mom's dagger stare made me stop midsentence.

Fine. I got up from the table, put my plate in the dishwasher, and headed to my room. It was Bronwyn's life. Let her be miserable. But I was definitely not going to find myself in the same unhappy place. So I pulled out a sheet of the stationery Grana had given me and wrote my own boyfriend list. It's both a wish list and a compass—something to prevent me from going in the wrong direction.

The first five items were easy to come up with—I wrote those down right away. The others came to me over the next few days as I listened to Bronwyn. It's a good list, and even though I've long since memorized it, I still pull it from the program once in a while to give it a read.

My Perfect Boyfriend Must:
1. Be cute.
2. Have good hygiene.

(If you knew the boys in my sixth-grade class, you'd know why I included this.)

3. Be smart, but not have to prove it (unlike Calla).
4. Be kind to people and animals.
5. Talk (but not flirt) with my best friend.
6. Be a good listener and take me seriously.

7. Not be sneaky.
8. Like to hold hands.
9. Take funny pictures together.
10. Give me surprises.

I glance down at my list. Gray checks off box number one, I think. And then I quickly catch myself.

He is a boy who's been in a terrible accident. He could die! This time, the knowledge nearly knocks me over like a wave. My legs go weak. What kind of person forgets something like that, even for a moment?

A terrible person, that's who.

I study my wall, looking for a particular quote.

> *Hope begins in the dark, the stubborn hope that if you just show up and try to do the right thing, the dawn will come. You wait and watch and work: you don't give up.*
> —*Anne Lamott*

I did the right thing by not leaving him, I remind myself—just like I promised. And now, I can't leave him out of my serious thoughts.

Mom pops her head into my room. "I'm heading to the hospital. Want to tag along?"

What? I can't believe she invited me at the exact

moment I was thinking about keeping my promise to Gray. I fold up the list and place it in my backpack along with Gray's sunglasses, and then I text Mari.

Me: Going to meet my destiny.

Will fill you in later!

Chapter 3

I'm actually shocked that my mother invited me to accompany her to the hospital. She never lets me tag along when she's doing her job. Maybe she thinks she needs to keep an eye on me. Whatever the reason, I slip on my flip-flops and jump into the front seat of our "on its last tires" Honda Civic before she can change her mind.

"Did you call your father?" she asks. My parents have been "amicably divorced" for two years, and they don't like us to keep the other in the dark about things. Calla says "amicably divorced" just means they don't bother fighting anymore. The weird thing is, I don't remember them ever fighting. "That's because you're the youngest," Bronwyn told me. "They stopped when you were little, long before the divorce."

"Yeah," Calla added. "Dad let Grana do all the arguing for him."

I've often wondered if that's true. Mom and Grana did argue a lot before the divorce, and they *still* can't be in the same room without getting on each other's nerves.

"Not yet," I tell Mom, and pull out my phone. "I figured he'd be in the gardens." But the truth is that Mari's texts distracted me.

My call goes right to voicemail. I start to tell my dad what happened, but there's too much. "Call me, and I'll tell you the rest," I say, and then I tuck my phone back into my pocket.

"How about Grana?" Mom asks, not so much suggesting as wondering.

I shake my head. "I'll let Dad tell her."

A little smile tugs at her lips. She probably thinks I'm just like her—avoiding my grandmother's judginess. But the truth is, for all our parents' rules about keeping everyone up to speed, Mom's happier when things stay between us for a little while.

You get to be an expert on things like this when your parents are divorced.

"So, are you okay?" Mom asks me as we turn onto the road through town. "You've been through a lot."

Her question brings me right back to the memory of finding Gray. I can't believe we're on our way to the hospital. That I might see him again.

I nod and sit up taller.

"What about the reporters' code of ethics?" I ask. Mom has told us many times that reporters, especially local reporters, must work hard to respect the privacy and dignity of those going through hard times. "Isn't showing up at the hospital an invasion of privacy?"

"This isn't just a story about an injured boy," Mom points out. "There was a hit-and-run."

"That's illegal, right?" I ask, gripping my seat belt.

"Precisely. Which makes this a criminal case, and one I have a responsibility to cover. My reporting could help the police find the person who did this heinous thing."

I do wonder who could hit a boy and leave him in the street to die. "If Gray's awake"—*please be awake*—"will you try to talk to him?"

"No. That would be crossing a line. But . . ." She leans toward me to share her plan: "Officer Dorian tells me that this case is now being handled by the state, and I'm figuring the state officer—who does have the right to talk to Gray and his family—will probably start at the hospital."

I feel the glow of being my mother's confidant. "Yeah, but will the officer talk to *you*?" People refusing to talk to reporters unless they're from big newspapers is one of my mother's most frequent complaints. I can't tell you how many times I've heard her say, "Everyone thinks our little newspaper is for gossip and advertisements, but how can I change that if they won't give me a scoop?"

"I think the officer will talk to me," she says.

"Especially when they learn that my daughter was the one who found the boy."

So that's why I'm coming along! Mom must really want to crack this case if she's combining work with family.

Midcoast Hospital is on the other side of Mussel Cove, nearer to where Dad and Grana live. It's a small hospital that Mom writes about often. She says that the hospital needs all the good publicity it can get to stay open.

Not only do lots of folks count on it for emergency care, but it employs more workers than any other business in this part of Maine. I know because Mari's stepmother works at the hospital as a medical technician.

My pediatrician's office is at Midcoast, so I've been there lots of times. (Mom insists we go to the doctor once a year, while Dad's more of a you-go-to-the-doctor-when-you're-sick kind of person. I'm firmly on Mom's side on this one: an ounce of prevention is worth a pound of cure, as they say.)

Mom parks in the shade behind the hospital, and we walk around to the front entrance. There's a large sign in the main hall that directs you to the right floor, but no one bothers to read it, because there's always a volunteer sitting at a desk directly beneath the sign who's happy to give directions.

"Ahmed!" my mother calls out to the man behind the desk. Ahmed used to be our babysitter before Bronwyn got old enough. "You're back at it!"

Ahmed lifts his head from a book and smiles widely at both of us. "Studying? Yup. Back in school. Dug enough bloodworms to get me another semester or two." Ahmed was only fourteen when he started watching us, but he's nearly nineteen now and just finished his first semester at UMaine. He turns to me. "How are you doing, little one?" That was the very first thing he asked me when we met, back when I was seven.

"Not so little," I say. That was the very first answer I gave him, and it applies more every year.

"And you're volunteering at the hospital again!" Mom continues.

"Thanks to you. This is my favorite place to study."

Dad calls Mom "the fixer" because she loves to solve problems. When Ahmed complained that he couldn't study in his crowded apartment and that our three-days-a-week library didn't have decent hours, Mom suggested this desk. "It's perfect!" she told him. "Once or twice an hour, someone will wander in with a question—usually they just need directions—and then you can get right back to studying."

"So, what can I do for you?" Ahmed asks us now.

Mom leans in. "Is Gray Olsen, the boy who was

the victim of the hit-and-run, still here?" she asks.

Still here as in *still alive*? Or still at Midcoast? When Grandpa had his heart attack, they moved him to Boston (where he died, though I quickly push that thought aside).

"I think he's still here," Ahmed says. "But I'm afraid—"

Just then, a frantic couple bursts through the front doors and rushes to the volunteer desk. Mom gently pulls me toward the front windows to give the couple a chance to talk to Ahmed privately, though their voices carry easily to where we're standing, just a few feet away.

"Excuse me," says the woman. She looks younger than Mom even though she has silvery white hair and is dressed very stylishly. "We're looking for our son. We were told they'd taken him here?"

Mom steps forward. "Mr. and Mrs. Olsen?"

The couple spins to see who called their names.

"My name is Tally Walsh. I can take you to the ICU," Mom says.

Mrs. Olsen takes a big breath and nods. "Thank you," she says, and then she and her husband follow Mom to the elevators around the corner.

I hesitate. I'm dying to tell Ahmed that I was the one who called 911. But this is probably my best chance at getting to see Gray, so I hustle to catch up with the others.

I get there just as the elevator door opens, but Mom motions for me to stay where I am. "My daughter was the one who called 911," she says to the Olsens just as the doors shut.

I freeze in front of the bank of elevators, watching the number next to the doors rise to three. I can't believe she's telling them without me! It's my story to tell, not hers. Besides, I want to talk with them, to find out what they know about Gray's condition and about the accident.

I shake my head and give myself a firm talking-to. Mom's trying to help, to get to the bottom of things. To do that, she needs to ask questions. If I were with her, Mr. and Mrs. Olsen would want to question *me*. I'd be a distraction.

Still.

I want to know what's going on. I deserve to know how Gray's doing, right? Mom said she may need me to help her talk to the police. Besides, I'm here to keep my promise to Gray.

Nothing is accomplished without action, I think. I press the elevator button and hop on.

Chapter 4

The elevator opens onto a waiting area with chairs and tables spaced apart for health safety. To the left is a large nurses' station, and to the left of that is a hall, which I'm guessing leads to patients' rooms.

Unlike the receptionists who sit outside my pediatrician's office and ask my mom if our address and insurance have remained the same, these nurses are bustling. They're looking at screens, and wheeling bags of fluid on poles, and passing clipboards to one another.

I don't see Mom or the Olsens anywhere. I suppose the Olsens are with their son. I wonder if Mom is with them.

"Hey, Peyton." It's one of the nurses behind the large desk, holding a bundle of files.

"Hi, Mr. Alvarez," I say, glad I remember his name. He's a friend of my dad's. "I'm looking for my mom."

He nods knowingly. I hope he's going to say that he'll take me to her. Instead, he says, "I'm sure she won't be too long. You can wait there." He points to the waiting area with his chin. "There's a TV."

I turn around to see what's on. It's a true crime show. Normally it would interest me, but not now. I'm bummed. I want to be wherever my mother is, with Gray, learning more.

I take a seat and look around at the six or seven other people in the waiting area, wondering why each of them is here. Who will get good news about a loved one today? Who will get bad news?

I hate that life can be so unpredictable.

An older woman who I think works at the IGA is looking up at the wall. I turn my head to follow her gaze. There's a large painting of three dinghies connected by rope, with their reflections in the water. Two of the dinghies face left, but one faces forward. The one facing forward is brighter, sharper than the others, though they're all on the same plane. I wonder why the artist didn't paint the other two as perfectly. It bothers me.

I look back at the woman, and she's looking back at me. She gives me a little smile, as if she thinks I need comfort.

A man a few seats down runs his fingers through his hair, and I realize that I know him, too. He's Mr.

Blake, the Brentwood camp director! I'm guessing from the look on his scruffy face that he's still waiting to hear if Gray is going to come out of the coma.

It takes me a minute to muster my courage, but I hobble over, hoping he'll notice my bad ankle, and sit next to him.

He looks up, and I can tell that he hoped I was an adult with news about Gray. I feel bad getting his hopes up. "I'm Peyton," I tell him, "Tally Cam—I mean, Tally Walsh's daughter."

"Of course!" he says in that way that teachers and principals, and apparently camp directors, do when they want you to believe that they know exactly who you are even though they don't. There're just too many kids in their lives, probably.

"Do you know how Gray is doing?" I ask.

For a moment, he looks really startled, but then he seems to recall that my mom's a reporter. But that's not why I know about Gray, and for some reason, I want Mr. Blake to know that.

"I found him in the road," I say, which sounds juvenile. I wish I'd said only the first part: *I found him.*

"Oh, God. That must have been awful," he says, taking off his glasses and rubbing his eyes.

His words make my eyes sting, reminding me once again that I'm not on a true crime show. Any moment now, we might learn that Gray has died. Mr. Blake holds out the tissue box that's on the table next to him.

I pull off my own glasses and squeeze the tissue against my eyelids.

We're both quiet.

Our shared feelings make me braver. "Do you know what happened—why he was on the road so early?"

Mr. Blake sits up a little taller. "Those two boys and their competitions," he says. "Three days ago, they challenged each other to see who could eat the most s'mores. They didn't stop until they were both puking in the bushes."

He seems to be happy to have someone to talk to. "Is that what they were doing this morning? Competing?"

"Yup," he says. "One boy in a kayak. One boy running on the road. Both trying to beat the other to Day's Donuts and back to camp. It's a miracle that the kid who took the kayak is okay. He'd never been in a boat before this week."

He looks up, realizes that others in the waiting area are listening, and stops. Then he lowers his voice. "I probably shouldn't have told you about the s'mores . . . or maybe even about this morning's competition. Do you think you can keep it between us?"

I nod, knowing he probably just remembered (again) who my mother is—it happens to me more than you'd think—and realized it's probably a bad thing for a camp director to admit that he doesn't have control over his campers.

"Okay, then. See you around," he says, and walks toward the elevators.

Then he comes back again.

"Scratch that, Peyton. I don't want you to keep secrets. My bad. You can tell your mother, or I will. She'll surely ask."

"Thanks, Mr. Blake," I say, and wish I could tell him that the accident isn't his fault. (But truthfully? It probably is. I mean, partly, right?) "I hope Gray wakes up soon," I say instead.

He gives me a small smile and leaves for good.

Still no Mom. I'm freezing in this air-conditioning. I rub my arms and then sit on my hands. Why didn't I think to grab my sweatshirt? I should make a list of things to have with me at all times. As Benjamin Franklin once said, "By failing to prepare, you are preparing to fail."

Scary music pounds in the background of the true crime show. Mr. Alvarez grabs the remote from a table and turns the volume off. Piano music streams into the room. I'm sure the music is intended to make us feel calm, but I find it irritating.

I look down to see what color my ankle is now: purple, heading toward black. I take a picture and text Mari.

Me: No news on Gray, but I saw his
parents!
Look at my ankle.

No immediate response.

I stick the phone back in my pocket and sigh loudly.

I'm getting really impatient. Where's Mom?

I decide to find her.

I wait until Mr. Alvarez disappears from the desk with the woman who was staring at the painting, then head down the hall like I know exactly where I'm going. The rooms have doors with glass windows, so I try to peek into each one without invading folks' privacy too much.

Omigod.

I see him. It's Gray Olsen, surrounded by machines.

I stand on the other side of the glass, staring. I talked to this boy, told him to hang on . . . and he did.

Mrs. Olsen is sitting beside him, staring off into the distance. I wonder where Mom is. I should probably keep looking for her, but I can't move.

He is a magnet for me. A powerful magnet.

We are connected, Gray and I, by an invisible cord. Think about it. One boy, racing to town, is hit by a car. One girl, racing to say goodbye to her friend, nearly crashes into him and calls for help. Maybe saves his life.

It could be chance, but it doesn't feel like it. Mom's always saying that everything happens for a reason, and maybe she's right. Maybe, as Mari says, Gray and I are destined to be together.

Star-aligned rather than star-crossed.

Chapter 5

It might sound weird to say that a boy in a coma is beautiful, but that's the only way I can describe Gray Olsen.

He has a bandage on his head and a bunch of wires and fluid flowing into his arm, but otherwise, he looks like he's sleeping peacefully, having happy dreams. Someone has tucked a well-loved stuffed dog in beside him. I wonder if he had the dog at camp or if his mother brought it from home. Either way, it shows that he has a gentle heart.

I just want to hug him.

Suddenly Mrs. Olsen stands, turns, and sees me peering in.

I feel caught—naked, even. For a minute, I consider racing in the other direction, but that would be absurd.

She comes into the hall, letting the door shut behind her. "Are you Peyton?" she asks.

I nod. "Sorry," I say. And I mean *Sorry for being here. Sorry for spying. Sorry he's hurt.*

"Don't be sorry." She walks right up to me and gently places her hand on my shoulder. "Your mom told me what you did. I want to thank you. Without you, Gray might not be alive." Her voice is softer and kinder than I expected from someone whose son was recently hit by a car and left to die.

"I wish I'd found him sooner," I say. "If only I hadn't dawdled, taken the time to make my bed—"

She stops me. "You saved him. That's all that matters."

"How is he?" The question slips out before I have a chance to examine it, make sure it's the right thing to say.

"The doctors don't know," Mrs. Olsen says, choking on her words. "He has several skull fractures. But sometimes children wake up after traumas like these. There's so much that neurologists still don't understand."

"He'll wake up!" I say, even though I'm the last one who would know. But I believe it.

Mrs. Olsen doesn't correct me. Her lips smile, but her eyes do not. "Could you do me a favor?" she asks.

"Sure," I say. "Anything."

"Would you keep an eye on Gray through the window? I promised my husband I'd return," she says. "He's downstairs talking to the police and the camp director. I'm letting him express all my anger for me."

I know there's no way adults would keep telling me these things if everything were normal. It reminds me of when my parents were getting divorced. It seemed like no one could keep their thoughts inside—Grana least of all. Everything spilled over, like bathwater when the tap's been left running.

"I don't mind watching him," I say.

"I know that the nurses are checking their monitors, but I'm superstitious." Tears well up in her eyes. "I'm afraid that if someone isn't watching, he'll slip away."

I nod, so happy to have a job, to be needed, to help in some way. And to get to be near Gray again. "I won't move until you come back," I say.

Now she really smiles. "Thank you for understanding."

I wait until she's partway down the hall before I peer through the window again. It's funny that Mrs. Olsen didn't ask me to sit by Gray's bed, but perhaps only family members are allowed in ICU rooms.

"Please wake up," I say quietly.

A muffled cough startles me.

I turn. It's not Mom. It's not a nurse. It's a kid about my age, maybe a little older, with hair that hangs in his eyes. He has stopped, no doubt surprised to see me standing there, looking in Gray's window.

Then he pivots as if he's just taken a wrong turn and keeps walking nonchalantly back toward the waiting area.

Chapter 6

The kid was only standing there for a moment, but I could tell from his messy hair and his careless expression that he's the type of kid who thinks life is just one big joke. I figure he must be the boy who raced Gray in the kayak. How could he look so unconcerned when his friend is lying in a hospital bed *in a coma*?

I glance back at Gray, who looks the opposite of the boy in the hall. He looks like he wouldn't harm a mosquito even if it was piercing his flesh. I can't help thinking of my boyfriend list tucked in my backpack. Number four: *Be kind to people and animals*. I have no doubt Gray meets this requirement, which makes this accident seem all the more unfair. Bad things shouldn't happen to people like him.

I wonder what he's dreaming.

Do people in comas dream? I start to take out my phone to look it up—and to update Mari—but then I decide to do it later. I don't want to take my eyes off Gray.

"There you are!" I turn to see Mom striding toward me. "I thought I told you to stay put."

You didn't really, I want to say. *You just held up your hand*. But then she turns toward Gray and softens.

"Such a tragedy," she says, and wraps both her arms around me.

We're both quiet for a moment. It's scary to think that Gray could still die.

She sighs. "The state officer wants to talk to you."

I'm about to tell her I can't leave, that I'm on official watch, when Mrs. Olsen returns with her arms wrapped around herself for warmth. She looks exhausted.

"Oh, here," Mom says to Mrs. Olsen, opening her bag and pulling out her wrap. It's made of the softest gray yarn and goes everywhere with her. The temperature constantly changes on the coast. Air conditioners are often set too high, or the sea blows in a gust of cool air from the north. It can be eighty degrees in the morning and fifty degrees by day's end.

Mom hands the wrap to Mrs. Olsen.

Mrs. Olsen looks like she's about to say no, thank you, but then you can tell she feels the softness. That wrap is like the warm sun peeking out from behind a cloud. She places it around her shoulders and relaxes for just a moment.

"I have to take Peyton down to talk to Officer Ku," Mom says to Mrs. Olsen. "But keep the wrap. I'll have one of my daughters come back for it tomorrow."

Not one of your daughters, I think. *Me*. I'm going to be the one to come back for the wrap tomorrow. It has to be me.

We get off on the second floor, a part of the hospital where I've never been, and walk down a narrower hall. I'm nervous. I can't help imagining one of those interrogation rooms you see on TV with a table in the center, a chair on either side of it, and a dim light hanging above it. I hope Mr. Blake already told the state officer about the boys' competition.

Mom knocks on a door. It opens, and I walk into a brightly lit room with chairs clustered in a circle. I imagine doctors talking to patients and their families in this room, but I could be totally making that up.

A kind-looking officer with a coffee cup greets us. "Hi, Peyton. I'm Officer Ku," he says, and directs me to a comfortable chair. Mom sits down next to me, which makes me very relieved.

"You've had a day, haven't you?" he says. "You did the right thing, stopping and calling emergency services."

"I nearly rode past him," I admit. "I thought he was a pile of clothes."

"Good for you for taking a closer look." He pulls out an iPad and begins tapping the screen. Then he looks up at me. His expression is still friendly. I don't feel like I'm in an interrogation room at all. "Can you tell me, Peyton, did you pass anyone else on the road? Anyone who might have witnessed the accident?"

I sit up taller. "I didn't see anyone," I say, "which is not so surprising, since the road isn't busy at that hour. But I did see Mrs. Lieberman out walking her dog. It's a . . ." I turn to Mom. "What kind of dog is that?"

Mom starts to think, but I realize it doesn't matter. "The dog's name is Chloe. Maybe she walked Chloe earlier," I say. "Maybe she saw the car."

Officer Ku smiles and taps at his iPad. *Wow*, I think. *Maybe in addition to finding Gray, I can help find the driver!*

"Do you know Mrs. Lieberman's address?" he asks.

I tell him. Just then, my phone buzzes with a call. Probably Dad. Unlike Grana, he won't mind if I call back later.

Officer Ku looks up at Mom. "We knocked on the door of 118 Winding Lane—the house closest to the accident—but no one was home."

Mom tries to figure out who lives in that house, but I beat her to it.

"That's the Langleys," I say. "They're summer people."

Officer Ku nods happily. "That's good to know," he says, tapping the information in. "Summer folks often install surveillance cameras."

I feel like I'm taking a test and getting all the answers right. I sit on my hands and sway from side to side. I want him to ask me something else.

He does.

"Do you remember seeing any debris on the road? Anything that might have come off the vehicle that hit him?"

An image of Gray's sunglasses in the pocket of my backpack flashes into my mind. Should I have left them on the road? But Officer Ku's question is about car debris, something that would help them find the driver. I think for a moment but come up empty. "I was so shocked to see a body—Gray, I mean—I don't think I noticed anything else."

"That's understandable," he says kindly.

But it feels like my grade just dropped to a C. Maybe he can tell that I'm disappointed in myself, because he says, "Don't worry, Peyton. We'll find the driver." Then he turns to my mother.

"Would you run this story as soon as you can? And would you please ask the public to help by coming forward with any information they might have?"

Mom nods, looking like she's the one who aced the test.

She ruffles my wavy hair as we leave the room. "Well done," she says, and then, *click!* She's onto the next thing: "Come on. I have a job to do."

Chapter 7

Mom gets a call just as we arrive home, so I go in ahead of her. Bronwyn and Calla are standing in the kitchen, having just returned from grocery shopping, and are arguing over a shirt Bronwyn is wearing.

"When are you going to cut it out?" Calla asks her.

The shirt is Dad's. Bronwyn didn't bring enough warm clothes to the farm last weekend, so he gave her one of his denim shirts to wear, and she kept it.

Bronwyn wears Dad's stuff like sports fans wear clothing with the name of their favorite team, and it annoys Calla to no end. She thinks it's Bronwyn's way of making it clear whose side she's on and of punishing Mom for leaving Dad.

For Calla, the only thing worse than our parents splitting up is the thought of us taking sides.

I know it isn't right to take sides, but I also don't think it's right to leave a marriage when you promised to stay.

"You're the only one who has a problem with it, Calla," Bronwyn says. "No one else does."

Mom comes into the kitchen, and the conversation stops.

"Right. Okay. Whatever," Calla says.

Mom gives Calla a little rub on her back. Once I heard her tell Dad that Calla has two settings: caring too much and not caring at all.

"Put the groceries away," Mom says to the three of us. "I have to file a story." She goes to the dining room table, opens her laptop, and begins typing madly.

I grab grapes and bananas from a bag and fill the wooden fruit bowl on the counter. "I had to talk to a state cop at the hospital," I say to my sisters, but they aren't listening.

"I'm starving," I say, realizing I haven't had lunch yet.

"Fix something," Mom suggests without looking up.

"Aren't you hungry?" I ask her, hoping that she'll whip up something for both of us.

She shakes her head. "I ate a lot of donuts this morning."

I turn to my sisters. "What did you guys eat?"

"Yogurt and berries," says Bronwyn. She grabs a handful of grapes and retreats to her room. Who knows when she'll emerge again.

I look at Calla. "Leftover spaghetti," she says,

making herself a glass of iced coffee from the leftovers in the pot. She's supposed to add more milk than coffee, but it looks pretty dark to me.

I'd forgotten about the spaghetti. "Leave me any?" I ask, staring into the refrigerator.

Of course the answer is no. Calla and I both love leftovers.

I fix myself a peanut butter and jam sandwich on whole wheat and eat half while standing behind Mom and reading over her shoulder.

I skim to see if she's included my name, but there's only one thing more certain than Calla eating all the leftovers, and that's Mom refusing to let our names appear in print or on social media unless it's for something school related. Lots of parents insist on keeping their kids' names out of print, but as a reporter, she has to be extra careful. Some people lash out at reporters if they don't like what they read, and some even threaten their kids.

She provides the details of the hit-and-run and then asks anyone who has any information to come forward.

"What if no one does? Come forward?"

She jumps at the sound of my voice. "You shouldn't be reading over my shoulder!" she says but answers my question anyway. "The police have ways of figuring out who the driver might be," she says, but

I can't tell if it's true or if it's just one of those things parents say to make the world sound like a reasonable place.

"Like what?" I ask, taking a bite of sandwich.

She turns to me, concerned. "I wish you didn't have to experience this," she says, sort of changing the subject.

"But how can—?"

There's a knock on the sliding glass door. It's Joey (or Ranger Joey, as Dad likes to call him) with his hands cupped to the window, peering inside. He lives up the road and is Calla's closest friend. Mom has told him a million times that he doesn't need to knock, but he always does. Perhaps it's because we're a family of girls.

Joey typically comes by way of the shoreline. Because he's wearing muddy boots, per usual, he leans into the house to say hi and to thank my mom for the umpteenth time for getting him and Calla jobs. They're helping surveyors count mussels this summer. It seems that the mussel beds in Maine are disappearing, and scientists are trying to figure out how many are left.

"I'll get my boots on and meet you out back," says Calla, and she heads to the mudroom off the front door.

"Hi, Joey," I say.

"Wear a hat!" Mom calls. "And sunscreen!" Then she gets up and grabs her bag. "I'm going to see if I can talk to someone who might have a clue who the driver could be."

"Can I come?" I ask, but she doesn't have to say a word. Her eyes tell me *absolutely not.*

I turn back to Joey, but he's gone, too.

So I pull out my phone and type into the search bar, *How do the police find hit-and-run drivers?* I'm looking at images of cars that have hit pedestrians—folded hoods, shattered windshields—when my phone buzzes with a call again.

It's Dad.

"Hey," I say.

"Hey, kiddo! You okay? What a horrible thing . . ."

"Yeah, I'm okay. Sorry I didn't call you right back. I was meeting with a state officer. I had to answer a bunch of questions."

"Seriously? Like what?"

My dad always gets excited by stuff he doesn't know, so I take my time telling him about the conversation I had with Officer Ku. "I think I may have been helpful," I say.

"Mom was there with you, right?" he asks.

"Yeah, definitely. I—"

"Hey, sweet pea." It's Grana, who must have grabbed Dad's phone. "What a day you've had! I can't wait till you get here tomorrow so I can give you the pampering you deserve. Your father is so proud of you."

"Thanks, Grana," I say. "I can't believe I—"

"It's Dad again. I can't wait to hear more tomorrow." I can detect frustration in his voice, but I know it's because of my grandmother's grabbiness, not because of me. "Tell your sisters I'll be there in the afternoon."

"Okay, Dad," I say, already looking forward to the time I'm sure to get alone with him.

We swap *love you*s, and he's off.

Chapter 8

Even during summer vacation, I try to rise earlier than Calla. The early bird and all that. And it's true. If I get up really early, I can have Mom all to myself.

I wash my face (circular motions), brush my teeth (two full minutes with my electric toothbrush), and brush my light brown hair (gently, so as not to split any of the ends). Then I find Mom, who is doing research at the dining room table.

"Hey, button." She puts her arm around my waist. "How'd you sleep?"

"Like a log," I say, which is surprisingly true. I thought I would keep seeing images of Gray lying in the road, but I didn't wake up once, and I don't even remember what I dreamed about.

"I'm sure you were exhausted," she says.

I nod. "What are you researching?" There are scraps of paper all over the table, and I take a moment to put them in neater piles.

"The percentage of hit-and-skips—that's what

some officers call hit-and-run accidents—that are solved." She hands me her coffee mug. "Would you mind giving me a warm-up? I'm putting the finishing touches on a second story for *BDN*."

That stands for *Bangor Daily News*. Mom is trying to get a job as a regular reporter for one of the larger newspapers. *BDN*, one of the largest in the state, has published a few of her stories, but they haven't offered a steady job.

I take her mug and fill it with more coffee (no sugar, no cream) and hand it back. Then I slide onto the chair next to hers. I'm a little chilly in my nightshirt, but the seat of the chair is already warm from the sun's rays. "I bet this story will land you a job there, Mom," I say.

"Let's hope," she says.

Her phone buzzes.

She stops typing to read the text. "I've got to run down to the grocery store. One of my sources saw a beat-up car abandoned in the IGA parking lot overnight."

"Do you think it might have been the car that hit Gray?"

"It's hard to believe the driver would leave the car right here in town, but it's the only lead I have." She quickly rereads what she's written in a mumble too low for me to hear. "Success," she says, which is what she always says when she presses send on a story. The word reminds her that writing the article is an accomplishment no matter the outcome.

As she stands and shuts down her laptop, I try to think of who her IGA source might be. "Was it Janine who told you?" I ask. That's my mom's friend from high school.

She smiles and hugs me from behind. "You are too smart for your own good." But it wasn't hard to put the pieces together. Mom has lived in this town her whole life. When Grandpa died, he left her the house she grew up in. Dad wanted her to sell it to help support the flower farm he owns with Grana, but Mom refused. Now it's where my sisters and I live Monday through Friday morning.

Mom scurries around, getting her glasses and her notebook. She dumps the rest of her coffee down the drain and sets the mug on the counter.

"You know, Mom, it takes about the same amount of energy to put the cup in the dishwasher as it does to put it on the counter."

Mom gives me her *hey, I'm the mom* look. Then she softens. "You're right, you're right. I probably won't be home before your dad gets here," she adds as she puts her mug in the dishwasher. "Are you packed?"

"About that," I say. "Can I stay with you this

weekend? I can help you try to find the driver."

"Absolutely not," she says. "It's my job to investigate and your job to resume your summer."

I'm tempted to say, "I'll get your wrap from Mrs. Olsen," but I'm afraid she'll think I'm obsessed with Gray Olsen and the accident (which I sort of am). Plus she might decide to get the wrap herself. It would give her a good excuse to see if Mrs. Olsen has more information about Gray or the driver who hit him. So I don't say anything.

She pauses at the door. "What will you do before your dad gets here?"

I think of a good reason for going into town. "I'll probably swing by the hotel and see if they still need towel folders. It won't be as fun without Mari, but it will be something to do."

"Good for you!" she says. "You may be surprised at how empowering it feels to go after something on your own."

I'm still thinking about her comment as she kisses me goodbye. Does she think I need someone else to motivate me? Most of the time, it's me trying to inspire Mari to be her better self, not the other way around.

"Bye, Mom!" Calla calls, suddenly appearing behind me. She squeezes past me and stands on the front porch.

Mom comes back to give Calla a kiss. "Glad you woke up so I can tell you to have fun this weekend. Remember to be packed when Dad gets here."

Calla groans, but Mom pays no attention.

It's not that Calla minds going to Dad's. She loves the farm. It's the packing she hates. No matter which house we're at, she complains that the item she really wants is at the other one.

"Make a list," I say.

"Mind your own business," she tells me.

I want to say, "Then don't whine when you forget things," but I decide to text Mari instead. I fill her in on all the Gray details, which makes me really excited to go to the hospital again.

Mari texts me back a string of hearts, and I wish I had asked her how things are going in Gloucester before going on and on about my life. A better friend would have.

I also wish I hadn't told Mom that I was going to the Anchorage. Now I'm locked in. She'll definitely want to know how it went.

I stand in front of the closet I share with Calla (my half arranged by color, her half mostly empty hangers with clothes piled on the floor) trying to pick out the perfect outfit for job seeking. I try to look cute, but not childish. Stylish, but not trendy. Fashion blogs suggest choosing a "signature look," but that's difficult when most of your clothes are your sisters' hand-me-downs. I have a cross of modern princess and natural scientist. It's hard to figure out who I am.

I choose a soft pair of cropped chinos (good for biking) and a cute blousy top. I put on sunscreen and reach for my backpack. That's when I remember Gray's sunglasses. I carefully pull them out and examine them. They have light frames and green-tinted lenses—in other words, very cool! I swear they tingle in my fingers, as if they're alive. My heart does a little skip. I pull off my own glasses and gently put on his. They're wobbly on my nose, bent from the impact. But still, I'm wearing something that belongs to Gray Olsen.

I think about sending a selfie to Mari but change my mind. Having these sunglasses in my possession feels private, like the promise of sharing something special with Gray in the future.

I stuff my water bottle, phone, and a few dollars into my backpack, pop on my fleece, and then grab my helmet and go.

I'm hardly out of my driveway when I realize that riding my bike feels different. I don't feel like someone who's been riding since I was seven. Instead, I feel like a kid who's just given up her training wheels. My wrists shake above the handlebars, and my knees feel wobbly. The potholes seem larger and more dangerous than they did yesterday. An approaching car feels as if it's heading right at me. My stomach lurches as it passes.

I wonder if my bike was damaged in the accident. But as soon as I think it, I know it's not the case. It's *me* that's different. Not my bike.

Breathe, I tell myself as I try to pedal a little faster. *You're just thinking about yesterday. Nothing has changed.*

There's rumbling from behind me—something big is barreling down the road! I quickly pull over to the side and stop.

A bus clatters by, making me flinch for no reason. A school bus.

One kid leans out a window and waves.

They're campers, I realize. It's the first-session kids heading back to Connecticut and places in between without Gray. I wonder if his friend, the one I saw at the hospital, is on the bus.

I'm not far from the spot where I found Gray, and I can't help pulling to the side of the road. I want to revisit the scene, to investigate more. I didn't see any debris around him yesterday, not in the middle of the commotion, and I'm sure the police searched the area for big car parts, but perhaps they missed something small. I might find something today. Something that could help solve this case.

There's a dark stain on the pavement. I shudder as I recall the bandage that was wrapped around Gray's head. Crows are hunched in the trees above me, cawing. No doubt they wish I'd leave so they can pop back down to do their own scavenging.

I decide to check a patch of trees in front of the Langleys' house to see if anything got thrown that far.

Right away, I spot a beer can. Maybe it's a clue. Maybe the driver was drinking. It's hard to believe that someone would've been drunk that early in the morning, but that could explain why they hit him—and why they kept going.

The can is heavy, so I tilt it a little to see if it's beer or rainwater inside. What pours out is pretty muddy. We haven't had rain for several days, so obviously the can has been here awhile. I set it on the side of the road so I can pick it up on the way home and recycle it.

There's nothing else in the trees, so I cross the street and search the roadside sand. There are cigarette butts, tossed by the clammers who park here during low tide, and a candy bar wrapper. Just when I'm about to give up, my sneaker kicks up something sparkly. I lean down and pick up a shard of glass. This feels like it could be a clue.

I text Mom, feeling good knowing I might be helping with her investigation.

Me: Are headlights made of glass or plastic?

> Mom: Plastic, usually. Why?
> Me: On my way to the hospital, found a
> piece of glass on the road. Is headlight
> of 🚗 at IGA broken?
> Mom: Hospital? I thought you were going
> to the hotel.

Ack! Ridiculous move on my part. Do I lie and tell her that's what I meant? Or do I tell her that I remembered her wrap and risk her telling me to skip the hospital? I do the right thing.

> Me: Both
> Mom: OK. But don't be intrusive.
> Me: 👍

Mom doesn't answer my question about the car. I tuck the piece of glass into my backpack and head off.

When I arrive at the hospital, Ahmed is not sitting at the desk. Instead, there's an older man I don't recognize. I give him a smile and walk directly to the elevators as if I have an appointment, which I sort of do. I have an appointment to get my mother's wrap back from Mrs. Olsen.

My heart flutters as I ride the elevator. Will Gray be awake? Have the doctors learned more? Are his chances good?

As I step into the waiting area, I notice the woman who smiled at me yesterday. I wonder who she's here to see.

At the nurses' station, I tell a young nurse with gorgeous beaded braids that I've come to see Mrs. Olsen. "Gray Olsen's mom," I add in case there's more than one Olsen in the ICU (which there probably isn't). I don't tell her that I've come to get my mother's wrap, because I'm afraid that then she'll volunteer to do it for me.

She tells me that Mrs. Olsen isn't here, but her husband is. "He's with the doctors," she adds. "Should I tell him you're looking for him?" She doesn't talk to me like I'm a little kid, and I like that.

"No, thanks," I say. "I need to see Mrs. Olsen. She borrowed something from my mother, and I'm supposed to retrieve it."

The nurse gives an understanding nod. "I think she returned to Connecticut to get some of more of her things," she says. "She'll be the one to stay with Gray for the long haul. But I'm sure she'll be back this weekend."

The long haul? Do they expect the coma to go on for a long time? This is the question I want to ask, but instead, I blurt out, "Is Gray okay?"

She hesitates for a moment and then says gently, "The same."

I think of asking her if I can see him, but this is probably what my mother meant by being intrusive.

What can I do?

Nothing. I should have worked harder to convince Mom to let me stay in town this weekend. I tell the nurse that I'll be back on Monday to see Mrs. Olsen.

She nods and turns her attention back to her computer.

I'm overcome by disappointment. Gray isn't awake. I didn't get to see him again. I don't even know if there's more or less hope that he'll wake up.

I don't usually pray, but I say a quick one for him, just in case.

From the hospital, I ride over to the Anchorage Hotel and pause when I get to the iron gate out front. It's a big hotel that sits on the harborside in the middle of town. I try to imagine myself working there, carrying towels to cute guys, asking if they'd like some water. It sounded like so much fun when Mari and I were planning our perfect summer. There are only a few jobs in Mussel Cove that kids younger than sixteen are allowed to have, and this is one of them. Bronwyn did it when she was thirteen, and she made a ton of money in tips. That sounded fun, too.

But now I don't have any desire to spend my summer behind these iron gates.

The only place I want to be is at the hospital with Gray. Nothing else feels important. Nothing else feels as real. It's as if my life has suddenly stopped, too. I'm suspended in my own weird coma.

Chapter 9

Dad doesn't pick up Calla and me until late afternoon. (Bronwyn, as usual, will be dropped off at the farmhouse later by her date.) We'd usually hear the motor of his boat, but we were watching one of those old-fashioned TV shows where people laugh at everything the actors say, so we missed it. (It made me sad when Calla told me that those were recorded laughs.)

"Why aren't you outside? It's a beautiful day," Dad says when he finds us.

"What's the sense in getting involved in something when you might show up any minute?" Calla asks.

"Good point," he says. "Next week, I'll try to give you a more exact pickup time." Shared custody: always a work in progress.

We grab our bags, head down to the small dock, and board *Silly Whim*, our dad's motorboat. Dad tosses us life jackets. We slip them over our heads and leave it at that.

"Clip up," he says.

Calla rolls her eyes. We've been swimming in these waters since we were toddlers. But there's no use arguing. We fasten our life jacket buckles.

"Do you want to drive, Calla?" Dad asks, knowing that I'd rather stare at the wake over the stern.

Calla, working hard not to show her enthusiasm, takes the wheel. She loves to drive everything: tractors, side-by-sides, snowmobiles. But she loves driving the boat most, and Dad knows it. He calls her the sea witch, which sounds mean but is actually an old family joke. When Bronwyn and her kindergarten friends played *Little Mermaid*, they'd let Calla join in if she took the part of the sea witch. She happily agreed.

We zip across the horseshoe-shaped harbor, past the village center (at the frog—or the middle—of the horseshoe, the part you hold). Mom's house is on the water on the right side of the horseshoe (closer to the frog than to the end) and the farm, Sea Spray Flowers, is at Bluff's Head, at the very end of the horseshoe on the opposite side. So if the tide is right, it's faster for Dad to pick us up in his boat than his truck.

I get a little sad as we approach the farm's dock. Mom always used to lean over the bow, to help direct, and Dad would say, "There can only be one captain of a ship." And then Mom would huff and let Dad maneuver until we were lined up correctly and could disembark.

Even though those moments were stressful, I miss Mom's voice every time we approach. The silence doesn't seem right.

Dad was never *really* a sea captain, but he does have more boating experience than she does. My parents met when Dad was the boating instructor at Brentwood Camp and Mom was working as a receptionist at the Anchorage. They married and lived in town over a gourmet market that Dad started. (Dad has always believed in supporting local farms.) Mom worked her way up at *The Notes* from the advertising department to reporter. Then Grana (who used to live in New Jersey) had the opportunity to buy the farm at Bluff's Head, and we moved in with her so Dad could pursue his dream of being a grower. You would think that living with Grana (who liked taking care of us girls) would've allowed Mom to go after her dream of being a journalist, too, but it didn't work out that way. Grana wanted Mom to "stop banging her head against the wall" and help grow the flower business. I suppose Dad agreed—he didn't say much about it.

Calla lingers at the water's edge, looking for signs of invasive green crabs that prey on mussels. Dad and I climb the hill, a blueberry field that's beginning to display berries that won't be ripe for a few more weeks. We pass a very small orchard of apple trees and then follow the mowed path between rows and rows of flowers that will be cut for farmers markets, bridal arrangements, restaurants, and the cart that sits at the end of the driveway where neighbors can leave money for a bouquet. Last weekend, there were only a few varieties blooming—tulips and daffodils, mostly—but this week the daisies, astilbes, and peonies are in full bloom. While Dad reframes one droopy plant, I hold a peony to my face and inhale. The petals are so soft, and the scent reminds me of clean laundry.

Dad says, "Did you know that peony plants can live to be a hundred and still produce flowers?"

"Wow. That's longer than most people live."

"I gave Mom a dozen peonies when I proposed," he says.

I nod. He's mentioned this before. I picture my dad holding a dozen of these big, showy flowers, and my heart aches for him. (I wonder if he knew that Mom's favorite flowers have always been poppies.)

He bends down and pulls a couple of weeds, so I follow. I use my finger to dig around the root of a dandelion showing that, even without a trowel, I'm committed to extracting these persistent plants the right way.

"I understand you wanted to stay in town this weekend," he says, changing the subject.

The way he says it makes me think that I hurt his

feelings. "It's not that I don't want to be here, Dad. I do. It's just that—I can't stop thinking about the boy who was hit. I want to do everything I can to help Mom solve the case."

A dark look comes over his face, and I worry that I sound too much like Mom when she's on the scent of a story. I can't help feeling like he'll love me less if I start sounding too much like my mother.

"That's Mom's job, investigating the story. You know that, right?"

I nod. "That's what she said, too."

"Good," Dad says. "Just so you're clear." He nods toward the birch grove. "I'm going to check out the hives." He's looking at me with expectation in his eyes. I know he'd love for me to say, "I'll come with you," but unlike my father, who is obsessed with all things having to do with organic farming, I find bees really boring.

As Bronwyn has pointed out, in the BD (Before Divorce) days, we could just do our own thing at the farm. But now that we only see Dad on weekends, there's this expectation that we'll spend all our time together, doing Dad stuff.

"Get yourself up here, Miss Peyton!" It's Grana, standing at the back door in her linen jumper. I give Dad an apologetic shrug and climb the steps to the stone patio to give my grandmother a hug.

"Something smells good," I say.

"Come see," she says, ushering me inside and lifting the lid on a Crock-Pot in the corner. "Vegetable stew. I'm mixing the cheese-and-herb dumpling batter now."

"Yum!"

"Right?" she says. "I bet your tummy's hankering for a slow-cooked meal."

I smile but feel a familiar tightness in my throat. I'm tempted to defend my mother by saying, "Mom grilled the most delicious burgers last night," but I don't. Instead, I think of another quote on my wall: "Take the high road. The view is better."

One thing is for sure: you always know where my grandmother stands on things. She's full of opinions and good advice. She can tell you the best way to organize your drawers, your notebooks, and your day. She'll tell you if an outfit looks good or if you should opt for something else that covers your trouble spots. She never sits down, and she often reminds us to keep going if we want to get somewhere in life. Sometimes I can't help wondering if things would have gone the way they did if Mom were more like Grana.

I've thought this ever since my parents called us to the green couch—which I now think of as the puke-green couch—to tell us they were getting divorced.

I sat between my sisters. Bronwyn cried immediately. Calla didn't cry, and although that gave me hope that maybe things weren't as bad as Bronwyn was making them out to be, it also made me sadder.

I don't remember everything. There was some talk about how people grow differently, and how Mom and Dad still respected each other, and how the divorce wasn't our fault. One thing I *do* remember was when Bronwyn asked, "Why can't you and Daddy just figure this out?"—which is exactly what they would say to us every time we squabbled: *Figure it out, guys.* The room went still when she asked that. It was if everything they'd said up to that point had been planned and now they had to think on the spot.

Dad spoke first. "*I've* tried," he said, and the way he said it made it clear that he didn't think *Mom* had tried. Not by a long shot.

Mom shifted in her seat and gave a little growl. And my mind scrambled for all of the ways that she hadn't tried hard enough. I thought of her distractedness, the way she'd leave a pot on the stove until its contents stuck to the bottom and took on a burnt taste, or the way she'd follow a news lead when she was supposed to be making flower deliveries, or how she clammed up when she was frustrated. And I realized that he was probably right. She *hadn't* tried hard enough.

Maybe Calla picked up on Dad's tone as well,

because she began pointing out some of his flaws. Like the way he always said he'd drive us to lessons and playdates but never did. Or the way he just walked away, ending a discussion, whenever he disagreed.

Mom said to Calla (and perhaps to Dad, too), "Nobody's perfect."

And I remember sitting there on that middle cushion, wondering, *Why not? Why not be perfect, or at least strive to be? It would take work, sure, but wouldn't it be worth it to do things right? Do it right or don't do it at all, as they say.*

That's when I vowed to put all my effort into being the best person I could be. I would read blogs and listen to Grana's advice. I would look my short-comings straight in the eye and correct them. How else could you prevent the pain of rejection? Or the knowledge that you had hurt others? I began collecting quotes and turning them into artwork for my wall. I have most of them memorized.

And when I get a little tight feeling that I get sometimes when I'm worried about how things will turn out, I think of what Grana would say: "Your happiness is up to you, Peyton."

Chapter 10

Here's the weird thing: even though we spend week-days with Mom and just weekends with Dad, the farmhouse still feels more like home. It's where I spent the first ten years of my life, learning my letters, drawing, playing games, and doing homework at the big kitchen table. It's where I learned to ride a bike, do a headstand, and recognize the summer constellations.

At the farmhouse, I have my own room, and Calla and Bronwyn share. I was a baby when we moved in with Grana, so my tiny room is still called the nurs-ery. Like my room at Mom's, there are pictures on the walls and knickknacks on my dresser and books on my shelves. But whereas the things at Mom's house were purchased all at once—she wanted us to think of Grandpa's old house as home, so she let us choose whatever we liked—the things in this room were collected gradually. The puffy cloth balloons were hung on the wall when I was one, and the porcelain bear bank on my nightstand was given to me by the grandmother I can't remember. There's a picture of me climbing my first tree taped to the mirror above my dresser. *Are You My Mother?*, the first book I ever read, is on these shelves, along with the entire Narnia series and Grana's dusty old copy of *Little Women*.

I'm thinking about the differences between my two rooms, how one is like a selfie and the other is like a scrapbook, when I crawl into bed. The cotton sheets are worn (just the way I like them), and the cricks and creaks of the house are the lullabies I know best.

There are sudden voices below: Bronwyn's home from her date. From my bedroom, I can hear every word spoken in the kitchen.

Dad: "How was the movie?"

Refrigerator opens. Bronwyn: "Okay. The ending wasn't that great."

I don't hear the rest, because I begin wondering about Gray and what it might be like to go to a movie with him. Mari says that boys always choose scary movies so their date will reach for their hand. I doubt Gray is like that. (Though I wouldn't mind holding hands. It's number eight on my list, after all.) I imagine us walking along and him asking, "What are your favorite movies?" I tell him that I like movies based on my favorite books. Then he nods, totally in agreement.

I wonder what books Gray likes to read. I get up and pull the boyfriend list out of my backpack. I add a number eleven: *Love Narnia.*

As I get back into bed, I decide I'll ask Mrs. Olsen if she'd like me to read to Gray. That would make me feel useful!

I go to sleep imagining myself sitting next to Gray, reading a book about time travel. Suddenly he opens his eyes . . .

My eyes open the following morning to bright sunlight and the sound of Calla practicing her mandolin. Dad and Bronwyn are calling back and forth in one of the gardens, probably cutting flowers for the farmers market in town. Typically I would be out there with them, completing my regular chore of weeding. (We have to do an hour a day on weekends. Calla and Bronwyn like to break their hours into smaller segments, but not me. I like the feeling of being done before breakfast.) But today, I couldn't wake up.

When I slink into the kitchen, I expect Grana to give me some advice about laziness, but she doesn't. Not this morning. She's going easy on me.

"You can help me pack this honey" is all she says when I appear downstairs.

We get to the town park early so Dad and Grana can get a spot on the sidewalk near the parking lot.

Folks usually stop at the first table that has something they want, so you can sell a lot more at the beginning of the sidewalk than at the end.

Already there's a crowd here, which means that the summer people are starting to arrive.

Bronwyn has play practice at the high school, so she can't stay. She buys a chocolate donut from Cecelia Hobbs (the woman who drove me home in her truck after the accident), eats half, and gives the rest to me. "See you later!" she says.

"Will you be riding back to the farm with us?" Grana asks.

"Probably not."

A cloud passes over Dad's face, but he doesn't say anything.

Bronwyn leans in to give him a kiss on the cheek. "Maybe we can play cribbage tomorrow morning?"

His face brightens. Bronwyn always knows the magic words.

Dad sets up tables in our booth and places the buckets of fresh-cut flowers around the base. Several other farmers pause to chat with him about rainfall, slug prevention, and green crab fertilizer. Mom and Dad's longtime friend Levi comes over to joke with Dad and to plan a bike trip together. They laugh heartily.

Grana smiles, and you can tell that she's proud of

Dad's enthusiasm for farming and the sheer number of friends who always seem to find him.

She and I arrange the bouquets and the honey on the table—something I adore doing. I slip a wilted daisy out of one bouquet and refasten the twine around it. Grana wraps her arm around my shoulders. I can tell she's pleased.

Calla pulls her mandolin out of the back seat of Grana's SUV and heads toward the other musicians who are playing today. Three different fiddle groups rotate Saturdays, but Calla knows all of them, so they usually let her play along on the songs she knows.

Once the tables are set up, Dad sends me off with a few dollars to pick out breakfast for myself. This is one of my favorite rituals. I walk from one booth to another, hearing, "Good morning, Peyton!" from all sides. I smile and wave to the people I know and check out the homemade options: bagels, croissants, egg pockets with goat cheese, cinnamon rolls, tarts.

I'm standing in front of the booth Cecelia runs with her husband, Bud, trying to decide if I want a raspberry pastry or a morning glory muffin when Lilliam and Jamie, two girls from my class, approach me.

"Hey, Peyton," they say together.

The three of us used to be close friends—BD. But it seemed like Mari and I just had more in common.

There's something comforting about being with someone else whose parents are divorced. Lilliam and Jamie (or L&J, as Mari nicknamed them) mean well, but after they heard about the divorce, they were always saying stuff like, "Do you get two Christmases now?" Like we'd choose that over having one with everyone.

"Have you been here long?" I ask.

"Not really," Jamie says. "We haven't picked out a treat yet."

"Did you hear about the hit-and-run accident?" Lilliam asks.

I nod. "I found him," I whisper.

"What?" Jamie squeals.

"I found the boy—Gray—in the road. He was unconscious."

Lilliam squeezes my arm. Jamie gives me wide eyes.

I purchase and share a large muffin as I tell the girls everything, including the fact that I have to go back to the hospital tomorrow and might read to him.

"What's he like?" Lilliam asks.

I can't answer, because that's when my father finds me. "Grana would like to get some breakfast," he whispers in my ear.

"I have to get back to work," I say. I can tell they're as disappointed as I am. And I decide that I should try to be a better friend and hang out with them this summer.

I'm headed to our booth, playing back my words to the girls and wishing I had remembered to tell them about the sunglasses, when I bump into someone. A guy.

"Hey!" he says. "Watch where you're going!"

"Sorry!" I say.

Omigod! It's Kayak Boy! The one who was at the hospital, standing in the corridor. He looks right at me with a jokey smile and then disappears.

Is his family staying in town?

I keep an eye out for him as I wrap bouquets, talk about flower care, and make change.

Grana returns and pulls out more event brochures from the car. Even though she can see that we're super busy, her retrieving them makes me feel as if I've fallen down on the job.

I'm making change for a customer when Grana mutters, "Damn fool." I look up to see who she's talking about.

Grana nods toward the musicians.

There's an old man in a hunter's jacket doing an exaggerated jig to the fiddle music right in front of the musicians. It's cute when little kids dance to the music, but this is awkward. I can't tell if he's making fun of the music or just wants attention.

Calla looks like she's afraid he's going to fall on top of her.

And then, as if all this isn't weird enough, a familiar figure jumps in and starts dancing with the old man. Yup, you guessed it.

Kayak Boy.

Chapter 11

The rest of the weekend is pretty uneventful, except for dinner on Sunday night, when Grana tells Calla and me that she's been cooking up a plan.

"Why don't you two live here for the summer?" she says, dishing out our favorite garlic mashed potatoes. "You can work on the farm, and we'll pay you. We would still need you to weed, but you can also help with the mulching and separating the bulbs. The two of you can manage the neighbor cart and take pictures for Instagram. Calla, maybe you could take over our account."

This is not a new plan. When Mom and Dad were getting divorced, Grana wanted summers at the farm to be part of the agreement. "After all," she said to my father (while we were in the room), "you only get the girls on the weekends. Tally gets them five days a week. Doesn't it make sense, girls, for you to spend summers with your father and me? Wouldn't you rather be on the farm in the summertime, just like always?"

"Mom," Dad was quick to say, "Tally and I will work this out."

Then, last summer, Grana suggested it again. We all pretended that it might be possible, but if Dad ever took it up with Mom, we didn't hear about it.

The truth is, we like living close to town. There are more activities, more friends, and there's less physical work. Besides, we might get five days a week at Mom's during the school year, but we're only home in the evenings.

"I already have a job," Calla tells her without even looking up from her plate.

"I'll pay you more than you make counting mussels," Grana says.

"Mom," Dad says, "we agreed that the girls would live with Tally during the week, year-round."

"I was speaking to Calla, David," Grana says.

Dad raises his eyebrows but doesn't say more.

"You have Martin," Calla says to Grana. "And Aunt Beth arrives soon." Martin is this year's intern, who started in May, and Aunt Beth is Dad's younger sister who comes to help every summer. She's ten years younger than Dad and Mom and a whole lot cooler. Martin stays in a yurt, while Beth stays in a guest cottage down by the shore.

I take a sip of iced tea, relieved that Calla is objecting to this plan. I definitely want to stay in town;

it's too far to bike to the hospital from Bluff's Head.

Grana sighs and turns to me. "How about it, Peyton? I'm sure your mother wouldn't mind if you worked here instead of at the Anchorage. We could really use your assistance."

I look to Dad for help, but he has tuned out.

"Let me think about it," I say, knowing that if I tell the truth about my resistance—that I am totally obsessed with a boy in a coma—they'll work harder to convince me to live on the farm.

Grana nods in a way that tells me that this conversation is far from over.

Monday morning. Back in town.

The weather forecast calls for rain later in the day, so I leave the house right after lunch, telling my sisters that I promised Mom I would ride my bike to the hospital and retrieve her wrap. (Mostly true—Mom just didn't think of it before she left.) I've got my copy of *The Lion, the Witch, and the Wardrobe* in my backpack so I can offer to read to Gray. I picture Mrs. Olsen saying, "How thoughtful of you. While you read, I'll get something to eat."

Ahmed has his head down, studying. I decide not to disturb him.

"How are you, little one?" he calls out as I pass.

"Not so little!" I call back.

On the elevator up, I rehearse what I'm going to say to get by the nurses' station, but when I step out, the same nurse with braids is standing nearby. She smiles when she sees me. "Mrs. Olsen's back with Gray this morning," she says, so I just head on back to his room, my heart fluttering like a hummingbird's wings.

When I get to his room, I stop and take the book out of my backpack, then sling the strap over one shoulder.

Peering in, I see Mrs. Olsen flipping through a book of her own, and my heart drops. Reading to Gray no longer feels like my special idea.

She looks up, sees me standing at the window, and waves me in.

I remember to sanitize my hands, then walk in.

The sound is different in this room—a more cushioned humming and the steady *blip, blip, blip* of the monitor. There aren't any balloons bouncing on the ceiling or flowers lining the windowsill, and I wonder if they're allowed.

I feel too shy to look at Gray.

"It's good to see you, Peyton," Mrs. Olsen says. "Grab that chair in the corner and bring it next to me."

I set my backpack and book on the floor. The chair has wooden arms and legs like the chairs in the waiting area and is too heavy for me to lift, so I drag it over. The scratching sound in this churchlike room seems so wrong.

When I have it in place next to Mrs. Olsen, I grab my book and lay it on my lap. Only then do I risk looking at Gray. He looks much like he did the last time I saw him, but his hands now rest at his sides, and the little dog is perched on the nightstand.

Mrs. Olsen glances over to see what I've brought and says, "I recognize that cover! Gray had to read that book for school last year."

"Really?" Mari's word, *destiny*, echoes in my head. "I was thinking I could—"

"He hated it. Said it was dreadfully boring."

I hold the book to my chest, regretting adding item number eleven to my boyfriend list. But maybe he never got to the best parts. Maybe he just doesn't love Narnia *yet*.

I'm about to ask Mrs. Olsen if she's learned anything new from the doctors (is that rude?) when she rubs her hand over the book she's holding. It's a photo book like the ones Mom made for each of us before she moved out of the farmhouse.

"I read somewhere that coma patients recover more quickly when they're reminded of stories from their own lives," she says. "That's why I brought this—so I can recall and share all of the wonderful stories from Gray's childhood."

I'm so relieved to hear hope in her voice. And it makes sense that if you tickle someone's brain with information about their life, they'd work harder to swim back to it. At least that's how I imagine it. I smile and lean over the book, hoping she'll tell me more.

"Look at this," Mrs. Olsen says. "Wasn't he the most adorable baby?"

The hummingbird in my chest flutters again as I glance down at the pictures. There's a picture of newborn Gray, baby Gray in a front pack, and then a picture of him in his high chair, leaning over and taking a great big bite of his first birthday cake—no silverware, no hands.

I have a picture of myself that looks exactly like this! I attacked my first cake the same way. We could be twins!

Mrs. Olsen turns the page and points to a picture of Gray around age four, crouching by the ocean.

"Gray," she says, leaning forward so he can hear her better. "Remember when we took you to Sanibel Island for the first time?" She has a smile in her voice. "We brought you to the beach, but you wouldn't leave the blanket. Not one step. Apparently you'd watched cartoons in the hotel room that morning and were suddenly afraid of quicksand."

I recall seeing cartoon characters sinking into quicksand. It was so frightening!

Mrs. Olsen keeps talking to Gray. "Remember, sweetheart? You called it 'tick-tan.' Daddy came up with a solution. He gave you a 'tick-tan stick' so you could test spots out before you stepped there."

I smile, and then we both stare at Gray, hoping to see some change.

Nothing.

Mrs. Olsen sighs and shuts the book. "I think I'll get a cup of tea."

"Do you want me to wait with him?"

"Do you mind?"

"I'd like to," I say, hoping that doesn't sound too strange.

"If the doctor comes by, tell her I'm in the cafeteria."

She shuts the door behind her, and my heart beats faster. I am in a room alone with Gray!

I study all the equipment surrounding him. I recognize the bag of fluid hanging on a pole. Bronwyn had the same thing—intravenous something—when she had her tonsils out. Wires attached to Gray's temple and fingertip lead to a monitor that's got wavy lines scrolling across it. Maybe it's a heart monitor?

What would I do if it suddenly stopped?

I push that thought away and decide to make

myself useful instead of just sitting here. I move my chair closer to the bed.

"Hi, Gray," I whisper. "I'm not sure if you recognize my voice. I'm the one who found you in the road. I called 911." I watch Gray closely as I speak, looking for any sign of awareness or understanding.

"I like your photo book," I say. "I was afraid of quicksand when I was a little kid, too. It's funny—quicksand didn't turn out to be the huge life problem I thought it was going to be."

Still, I think, how scary. I imagine myself slowly sinking into the ground without any way to stop it.

I shift in my chair. "Come to think of it," I murmur to Gray, "real-life problems sort of surprise you like quicksand, don't they? Like when my parents said they were getting a divorce. I mean, one day we were a family, and the next day we weren't. My whole life as I knew it was sucked out from under me."

The monitor beeps more loudly.

Omigod! Was that a reaction from Gray?

Chapter 12

Apparently it's normal for heart monitors to beep loudly sometimes. A nurse popped in, made sure that all was well, and then left me with Gray again. I can't wait to text Mari all the details.

It's not until I park my bike in the garage that I realize that not only did I forget to ask Mrs. Olsen for the wrap, but I also rode right by the Anchorage without stopping to ask for a job. I could go back, but it's starting to cloud over.

Do I tell Mom the truth? That I was so caught up in thinking about Gray that I didn't for one moment think about anything else?

As it turns out, I don't have to worry about preparing an excuse.

The sound of clippers coming from the open window tells me that Mom is in the backyard, hacking at the *Rosa rugosa*s growing around our deck.

This is never a good sign.

*Rosa rugosa*s are super thorny and grow pretty

aggressively, like monster plants. Cutting them back hurts—you can't avoid getting scratched, even if you wear long sleeves and leather gloves—and removing them is nearly impossible. My mother only tackles the trimming when she feels as ferocious as they are.

And she only feels that ferocious when she's angry. (Once, when Dad agreed with Grana that Mom couldn't accept an opportunity to interview Malala because they had to prepare the farm for opening weekend, Mom vented her frustration by clearing the brush encroaching on the orchard. She did it with a chainsaw.)

"What's going on with Mom?" I ask. My sisters are lying on the living room floor, listening to the latest *Dear Hank and John* podcast.

Bronwyn shrugs.

"*Rosa rugosa* is an invasive species," says Calla. "She should just get rid of it once and for all."

Neither of them seems especially concerned, so I can assume they're not the source of Mom's fury.

It could be Dad, I suppose. Maybe Grana has ramped up her campaign to have me come live at the farm? Maybe Dad's supporting her? That would make me want to hack some bushes, too. I open the sliding door and head out to offer my moral support.

"What did those poor roses do now?" I ask Mom as she continues to decimate the tops.

She stops clipping and pulls out her earbuds.

"Everything okay?" I ask. "Did Dad call? Or Grana?"

She looks startled. "No. Is there something you need to tell me?"

I shake my head. "I'm trying to guess why it's rose-trimming time."

She chuckles. "You're too funny!"

She sets the clippers down and pulls off her gardening gloves, then sits on the deck steps and takes a long drink from her water bottle. "I'm frustrated with the Olsen case," she says. "I received two emails from people who confessed to being the driver of the vehicle."

"You did?" I leap over the steps and onto the ground, then turn to face her. "What did you do? One of them has to be lying, right?"

"Both are. I took time out of my day to interview each of them—so excited that they wanted to talk to me before going to the police—but neither one's story added up. They got the details all wrong."

"And that made you mad?" I ask, surprised that this setback would bother Mom so much. I want to quote Ralph Waldo Emerson—"For every minute that you are angry, you give up sixty seconds of peace of mind"—but I decide against it.

"I'd already told two major papers that I'd have a lead story by the end of the day."

"Oh." I feel bad for her. She's wanted to be a reporter for a major paper since I was a little kid.

She sighs. "That, and I was feeling so relieved that the driver wasn't local."

I chew on this for a moment. It never occurred to me that the driver could be someone who lives right here in town. Or, quite possibly, right here on our road. That would definitely make the reporting a lot harder for Mom. I sink down on the steps next to her. The rose smell makes me feel light-headed.

"That doesn't make sense," I say. "Why would anyone confess to a crime they didn't do?"

Mom pulls a sweaty strand of hair off her face. "Believe it or not, it happens all the time. The reasons are complicated."

I brush a mosquito off my leg, hoping it won't be back. My determination to save lives never lasts long in our mosquito-infested backyard. "Maybe you could write about that? False confessions?"

Mom looks at me, but it's clear that she's deep inside her brain. "That's not a bad angle," she says. "It would be one way to present the facts again and request that people with real knowledge come forward."

"And confessing to a crime you didn't commit is interesting," I say. "I'd read that article."

Now she really looks at me. "When did you get so brilliant?" she asks.

I want to stay here with Mom on the back steps forever, basking in her praise, but she's feeling calmer, so she's already on to the next thing. *Click!*

My sisters are in the kitchen, trying to figure out dinner. One of their favorite things is putting together random ingredients to make something tasty. "We have canned tomatoes and a sweet potato," Bronwyn says, her head in the pantry.

Calla puts these ingredients into a Google search. "Do we have peanut butter? If so, we can make African peanut stew."

"We do," says Bronwyn, pulling it off the pantry shelf.

"That sounds exciting!" Mom says, looking over Calla's shoulder.

Calla shoots me a look that says, *Don't tell Mom that Grana made this for us once.*

I give her a face that says, *I know better than that.*

"We don't have kale," Mom says, "but your dad left spinach from the kitchen garden." She sits down at the table across from Calla to start her new article.

My phone buzzes. It's Mari. She's texted a selfie with a very cute guy she met at a barbecue. He's trying to take a bite out of her s'more and already has marshmallow on his face. Apparently his name is Jared, and he's painting a house down the street from her aunt's.

Me: Cuuute! How old is he?

Mari: Idk! Haha! Maybe 14?

Me: Have you hung out much?

Mari: A few times. He stops by on his breaks to see if the twins and I are playing outside. He's SO CUTE, isn't he?

Me: Be careful! Remember: fine feathers don't make fine birds.

Mari: Or maybe they do 😁

It's weird—I should feel so happy for her. But I'm reminded that this was going to be the summer of *our* first boyfriends, that we were going to spend all our time together folding towels and sharing details. It was as much about *us* as the boys.

But then I recall my morning with Gray and think maybe we *are* having this experience together. So I fill Mari in on the details. I tell her how I learned that even though Gray's in a coma, he can probably still hear people talking to him, and about the scare I had when his heart monitor beeped while I was talking to him, and how I made a promise to him when I found him—that I wouldn't leave him—and I intend to keep my promise.

No text back. She probably got called away.

So I offer to help my sisters, who give me onions to chop. I pause three times and look out the window to keep myself from crying. I notice the clippers Mom left on the lawn and think about what she said.

I've been thinking of the hit-and-run driver as a total stranger, someone from far away. But our road isn't traveled by many people outside the neighborhood. There are no public beaches or trails around here, and no businesses other than Brentwood. The road dead-ends at the Brentwood beach. Mom has probably realized that the criminal is likely one of our neighbors or someone visiting one of our neighbors.

Secrets are being kept.

I think about the salts—the folks who leave early for work. Maybe the driver overslept and was racing down our lane to get to work on time.

But as I start to mentally list some salts, I realize that it could just as easily have been a pepper, someone who was really tired after a night shift. And maybe, after their long night, they had a drink or two. Maybe the driver was drunk and doesn't even know they hit Gray.

Salts would've been going toward town. Peppers would've been returning home *from* town.

While Bronwyn and Calla argue over whether the sweet potato has to be cooked ahead of time, I leave the chopped onions on the counter and slide into the chair next to Mom.

"Do the police know which way the driver was going when they hit Gray?"

She stops typing and thinks. "I'm not sure. But I'm guessing his injuries might indicate whether he was hit from the front or from behind. Why?"

"Well, couldn't you figure out who might've been coming or going down Winding Lane at that hour of the morning?"

She thinks for a moment. "I don't know. That could be tricky. I mean, someone might have had an early-morning exercise class or driven most of the night to get to their summer home. And even if I could narrow the possibilities, then what? I can't very well knock on doors and ask."

I get up and pour everyone a glass of seltzer and think some more.

She could check out the cars of those drivers, though. For damage. Well, maybe Mom the reporter can't . . . and maybe the police can't. (I bet they'd need search warrants.) But perhaps a twelve-year-old girl can.

I picture myself saying to Gray soon after he wakes up, "My mom broke the story about the person who hit you, but I was the one who solved the case."

How's that for a perfect love story?

Chapter 13

"I'm going for a bike ride," I tell Mom the following morning as she gathers her things to head out the door. "For exercise."

Bronwyn and Calla haven't even opened their eyes.

"You could get some extra exercise," Mom says, "by picking up those rose branches I left all over the backyard and carrying them to the compost pile." She's got a big grin on her face.

"Maybe," I say, thinking that I don't really want to put on pants and a long-sleeved shirt to move them. "But I have a big day today."

"Oh?" She stops in the middle of leaning toward me for a goodbye kiss.

"I'm without a doubt going to the Anchorage today," I say.

"I thought you went—"

"And I'm going to stop by the hospital and get your wrap."

Mom kisses me. "I forgot about my wrap. But no need. I'm going to stop by the hospital today. I'll get it myself." And she's off.

Ack! I knew I shouldn't have told her. I knew she'd tell me not to bother. Now I have no solid reason for seeing Gray again. Or do I?

I pick up my backpack and check the bottom pocket. The sunglasses are still there, along with my boyfriend list. If I need an excuse, I'll just tell her that I was returning the glasses.

I very quietly grab a little notebook from my bedroom and my grandfather's field binoculars from the chest in the living room, then slip out the door.

I designed my investigative pages last night before going to bed. I have a chart to record names, occupations, whether the person is likely to have been driving at night or in the daytime, and the condition of their car.

I decide to head toward Brentwood Camp first. There are way fewer houses in that direction, and I can do the other direction on my way to or from the hospital—I mean, the Anchorage.

I can skip the first house, Cecelia Hobbs's, because I know her truck is in fine condition.

The next house belongs to the Dales, an elderly retired couple. Mr. Dale takes his wife (who never drives) out to breakfast every morning, but not super early. Still, Mr. Dale could have a regular sunrise habit. I decide to leave no one off my list.

Their car isn't in the driveway, so I lean my bike against a birch. Staying close to the tree line, I scoot around to the back of the garage, hoping it has windows. Yes! I should be able to examine the front of their Subaru head-on.

I stand on tiptoe to peer in. It takes a minute for my eyes to adjust, but eventually I can see the hood and the headlights pretty clearly.

No damage detected. I record my findings and get back on my bike.

The next little house, on the opposite side of the road, belongs to a youngish clammer named Eb Gordon. Well, it doesn't really belong to him—he rents it. But he's been here as long as we have. He backed his old Jeep into the driveway, so it's easy for me to check out the condition of the front end. I stay where I am, across the lane, and take out the binoculars. In case anyone is watching, I look up first, as if there's a rare bird in a tree near his cottage. Then I swoop my gaze down, as if the bird just flew away.

The Jeep is pretty banged up, but nothing like the mangled vehicles I saw on the internet. Besides, most of the dents on the side I can see are rusty. And not just a little rusty—*very* rusty. Like they've been there a long time. And if he did hit Gray, wouldn't he keep his car parked facing his house?

I'm feeling like a full-fledged detective as I fill in the boxes of my chart.

I record what I can at the next two houses, the Ingalls' (she's a housekeeper, and he's a chef) and a summer couple's. But none of their cars are on the properties. After that, the houses become scarcer.

I ride along at the edge of the woods for a bit, daydreaming of Gray. I imagine whispering to him, "Don't worry: I'll find the criminal who did this to you."

A chipmunk runs out in front of me, and I totally overreact, nearly flipping my bike. Guess I'm not entirely over my jumpiness.

I pull over and take a moment to catch my breath.

A glimmer of ocean sparkles through the trees; it's high tide. And something else is glimmering, too. Something in the woods.

I want to investigate, but there's a no trespassing sign on a tree a few feet away. Even though, as Calla says, the signs have been put here to deter clammers from parking on the road and making their own path down to the shore, they still make me nervous. If I step onto the property, I'm kind of breaking the law, right?

"It is a good idea to obey all the rules when you're

young just so you'll have the strength to break them when you're old." Mark Twain said that.

Don't be silly, I tell myself. There's a difference between doing the right thing and being a baby. And in truth, I've already trespassed lots of times this morning. At least here in these woods, no one is likely to care.

I set my bike down and head toward the sparkly object.

I find a bike tucked behind a fallen tree. It's an old-style bike (no gears), but it's in fairly good condition. It definitely has less rust than Eb Gordon's Jeep. And it's adult-size.

A shiver comes over me. Is the rider in the woods now?

I scurry back to my own bike, pulse pounding, and run through the possibilities. The tide is still fairly high, so it's not a clammer. Someone could be fishing on the shore. Or maybe foraging for fiddleheads and mushrooms. Either way, *they're* trespassing.

I jump back on my bike and head to the last two houses before Brentwood. The first is the Parson place, which is a summer rental. There are no cars in the driveway, and there's no garage. Check!

I've never met the woman who lives in the last house, Mrs. Wagner. Mom thinks her family owned most of the land on this point at one time. Sometimes

I see her driving an old but fancy car. She never waves, and she never comes to the neighborhood parties, either. Well, not since her husband died.

To avoid being seen, I ride farther down the road and lean my bike against a meandering stone wall. I take a moment to fill in the next row of my chart. Name: Mrs. Wagner. Occupation: none (at least that I know of). Then I creep behind her outbuildings—a barn, a shed, and what my mother calls a carriage house—hoping that I'll luck out like I did at the Dales' and there will be windows on the back side of her garage.

There aren't.

I backtrack to the side window, hoping I can still get a good glimpse of her car. If the hood is all pushed in like so many of the images I saw online, it should be obvious.

"Just what do you think you're doing?"

Omigod! I feel like I just fell out of a tree and can't catch my breath. I bend over, thinking it might help. "You scared me!" I say, still folded over, trying to buy some time now.

"Good!" Mrs. Wagner says.

I straighten up and say, "I'm Peyton Campbell. I live down the road."

Mrs. Wagner is surprisingly tall, with very short gray hair and piercing eyes. Her spindly hands are wrapped around a coffee mug. "That doesn't answer my question."

I suddenly recall a time when Cecelia Hobbs came poking around our garage, and I provide a similar explanation to hers.

"The Hobbses' cat is loose again and hasn't come home." I get all of this out with only one little catch in my throat. (I swear my throat always closes up when I lie.)

Mrs. Wagner squints as if she's sizing me up.

"Sometimes cats get trapped in garages," I say, trying to sound knowledgeable. "People don't realize they've closed the door on them."

"And just when did this cat get loose?" she asks.

"The day before yesterday." I hope I sound convincing.

"Well, I can assure you that the Hobbses' cat is not in my garage," Mrs. Wagner says, then takes a sip of her coffee. "My car has been in the body shop all that time."

Omigod! The body shop? Isn't that basically an admission of guilt?

Chapter 14

I stand up even straighter, trying to steady my breathing all over again. "Oh," I say, as natural as day, "did something happen to your car?"

Her eyes smile over her coffee cup as she takes another sip. Then she lowers the mug and says, "Haven't you done enough snooping today, Miss Campbell?"

It gives me the chills. Like she knows that I know. I feel like turning and running before my body ends up in her basement or something.

Stay calm, I tell myself. *Be brave*, I tell myself.

"Well, let me know if you see the cat," I say, and walk back to my bike, trying hard not to step on any of the flower beds that dot her front lawn.

I can't get on my bike and out of view fast enough.

As soon as I'm around the bend, I pull over to call Mom. The call goes straight to voicemail. Maybe she's at the hospital. I remember seeing a sign in the ICU hall that said NO CELL PHONE USE. So maybe she's turned her phone off. I hang up without leaving a message. What I have to tell her is too important to leave in a voicemail.

I hop back on my bike and speed toward town.

When I get to the hospital, I drop my bike on the newly mown lawn (I should recommend that they get a bike rack), wave at Ahmed as I race past the information desk—"Sorry, I'm in a hurry!" I call over my shoulder—and take the stairs two at a time.

Thankfully my ankle is no longer achy. But I'm out of breath when I pull open the heavy door to the waiting area.

I try to compose myself and act like I have every right to be here as I stride right by the nurses' station on my way to Gray's room.

When I peer through the window, Mrs. Olsen is sitting alone, holding the hospital phone to Gray's ear, even though he's still not awake. I'm surprised; I was so sure Mom would be here.

Mrs. Olsen looks up and waves me in.

I hesitate. I really want to tell Mom what I discovered, but I can't resist the chance to spend time with Gray again.

I send a quick text to Mom.

Me: Breaking news! Text me when you can!

There's no immediate response, so I turn off my phone—per the sign in the hall—pop it back in my pocket, and go into the room.

Mrs. Olsen says goodbye to her husband and promises to call regularly.

The monitor in the room is making its familiar beeps.

"Hi," I whisper. "Any change?"

She shakes her head and pats the chair next to her. My mother's wrap is folded on the seat, so I pick it up and place it on my lap.

"Mom was going to come by and get this," I tell her. "She hasn't been here yet?"

She shakes her head again.

I am so tempted to tell her about my run-in with Mrs. Wagner, but it feels disloyal to tell anyone before my mother.

I lean over and say, "Hi, Gray. It's Peyton again." I stare at him to see if I can detect any response. Maybe his eyelid moved?

Mrs. Olsen places her hand on mine.

"Have you been telling Gray more stories?" I ask her.

She nods. "I reminded him of his first day of pre-school. I was worried that he'd cling to me, that he wouldn't want to stay. Instead, we got to his class-room door, and he turned to me and said, 'I've got it now.' And I told him about how he got a triple play one time in Little League." I ask her what a triple play is, and she describes how Gray caught a grounder and proceeded to get players out on all three bases.

She tears up at the end of this story and goes to get a tissue.

I think about Gray's spectacular play. I don't know much about baseball, but it sounds like an intelligent move. Check item number three—*be smart*—on my boyfriend list!

It takes Mrs. Olsen a few moments to regain her composure, so I pick up Gray's photo book and glance through it. "Hey!" I say. "I had a windup frog exactly like this one!"

"Gray had oodles of windup toys," Mrs. Olsen says. She comes back, sits down, and finds a picture of his collection in the book.

I wish I'd collected more. Maybe it's not too late to start. Maybe Gray and I can surprise each other with them! (Number ten on my list.)

Mrs. Olsen tells Gray a few more stories, and then Mr. Alvarez comes in with a physical therapist, who's here to move Gray's muscles. Apparently this can also help the communication system in his brain. Mr. Alvarez excuses himself, and Mrs. Olsen grabs her purse. I scoop up my mom's wrap and take one more peek at Gray before readying myself to leave, too.

But instead, Mrs. Olsen pulls out a handful of dollar bills. "Would you mind getting me a muffin and some tea from the cafeteria, Peyton?" she asks.

"Sure!" I say, thrilled to be useful to her. I tuck the money into my pocket, set the wrap back on the chair, and practically sprint through the waiting room.

According to the elevator buttons, the cafeteria is on the second floor. The door opens, and I follow the signs. The windows of a gift shop catch my attention. There are some cool-looking games and puzzles in the window. I pause for just a second, wondering what I might surprise Gray with when he wakes up—*if* he wakes up? No! Not *if*, *when*—but then I remember my task.

The cafeteria is large and far more attractive than the one at school. The lighting is dim in a soothing way, and there are lots of plants all around. There's a large buffet in the middle of the room with other food stands scattered around.

As I'm looking at all of the amazing choices on the buffet, I realize that I never ate breakfast. I check my backpack to see how much money I have tucked in the hidden pocket. Looks like I can buy one thing, as long as it's small.

"Are you buying?"

I look up.

Omigod! It's him! Kayak Boy!

Then his question registers. Am I buying? Is he serious?

"Absolutely not," I say. Certainly not for *him*!

He smiles and reaches for a bagel-and-egg sandwich and places it on his tray. "This is the third time I've seen you," he says. "Second time at the hospital."

"Are you here to see Gray again?" I ask.

He seems startled by my question. *Taken aback*, as Bronwyn would say.

"Who said I was here to see Gray?" he asks, grabbing a second bagel sandwich. "I don't even know a Gray."

He's not convincing. Not for a moment.

"You were coming down the hall to see him the other day."

He holds a yogurt in midair. His fingernails are filthy. (I think of number two on my boyfriend list: *Have good hygiene*. Massive fail!)

"What makes you think you know anything about me?" he asks.

I grab a blueberry muffin for Mrs. Olsen. Everyone likes blueberry, right? "I know that you were the one racing him—the one in the kayak."

He looks at me like I'm off my rocker, and I realize that I don't know this for sure. But if he's not Kayak Boy, then how does he know Gray?

His shoulders relax. He even chuckles a little. "You're wacked!" he says to me. Then he picks up his tray and walks up to one of the cashiers.

What? *I'm* wacked? He's the one who suddenly changed his mind and did that pivot in the hall!

I quickly locate the tea, then pay and follow him into the seating area.

I'm about to overtake him and force him to confess to knowing Gray when he takes a seat across the table from an older man. It's the same man I saw at the farmers market, dancing his odd little jig!

Now I'm *really* curious about this kid. If he wasn't the one in the kayak, he must be a summer kid. Probably a first-time renter, since I haven't seen him before.

I'm tempted to linger at a nearby table, out of sight but within earshot, but the boy and the man seem to be in no hurry at all. And I need to take Mrs. Olsen her tea.

I head toward the elevators, and only then do I realize that I forgot all about my breakfast sandwich.

Chapter 15

"Sorry it took me so long!" I say to Mrs. Olsen when I get back to the room. "I bumped into someone."

"No worries," she says as I hand her the tea, the muffin, and her change.

"It's blueberry," I tell her.

"Gray's favorite! And one of mine, too." She sets everything down on the counter and hands me my mother's wrap in exchange. "I can't thank you enough for coming by, Peyton," she says. "You are a comfort."

I guess it's time for me to go. I pull my backpack straps tighter, like I was preparing to leave at this very moment all along. "Coming here makes me feel optimistic," I explain.

She gives me a little hug. "I hope Gray can meet you properly soon."

The way she says that turns my body into rippling waves. I mean, first, it means that she believes that Gray will wake up soon. And second, she's got to think we'd be great friends (or more than friends) if she's saying something like that!

I nearly float to the elevators and toward the main entrance.

"Goodbye, Peyton!" Ahmed calls from the information desk.

"Ta-ta!" I call as I wave.

I tuck the wrap into my backpack, pick my bike up off the hospital lawn, and mentally tick off my morning accomplishments: (1) possibly solving the hit-and-run! (2) getting Mrs. Olsen's tea, (3) retrieving my mother's wrap, and (4) receiving a compliment from Mrs. Olsen.

I haven't heard from my mother, who's probably busy reporting, so I decide to add one more thing to my list of achievements: asking for a job at the Anchorage. Failing to ask feels like a task unfinished. "Live now, do now," as one of my favorite T-shirts says.

I slow my bike down as I enter the hotel gate and park it in the rack. There's a tickly little breeze. I can smell the salt air. I walk past rose gardens and benches and enter the large and elegant lobby. "Try, Try, Try," the number-one song of the spring (and Mari's and my favorite), is playing over a speaker. *"You gotta try, try, try to fly, fly, fly,"* I softly sing along. It makes me sad that Mari's not here. This is something we were supposed to do together.

There are tons of people in the lobby, and I hear snatches of French and what I think might be Italian.

One woman, holding a miniature poodle in her arms, asks the doorman about the fireworks on Thursday night. I had completely forgotten that the Fourth of July is this week.

If only Gray would wake up in time! I imagine finding a wheelchair and sneaking him onto the hospital roof so we could watch the fireworks over Mussel Cove together.

The desk clerk, who seems like a college student—probably the same age my mom was when she started working at the hotel—is dressed in a crisply ironed white shirt. I look down at my own clothing. I'm definitely not looking as nice as I was yesterday. Maybe I should wait, come back tomorrow.

"May I help you?" the desk clerk asks.

Too late. I step up to the front desk and affix my most professional smile to my face. "I was wondering if you still needed towel folders this summer."

"You mean junior hosts?"

I nod, wishing I'd remembered to use the official job title.

"I don't think so," she says. "I think Mr. K—the manager—hired the last one yesterday."

Yesterday! I wonder if it was before or after I planned to stop by. It's funny—I was almost hoping that I wouldn't get the job, but I still feel disappointed. Like I've let my nearly thirteen-year-old self down. Now I might never be a junior host, and I have only myself to blame. (Well, maybe Mari, too.)

"Mr. K isn't here right now," she adds. "He's at a funeral today. But you could stop back tomorrow and talk to him if you want."

"Thanks," I say.

"You should definitely come back," she says. "It's a fun job."

I think she's trying to cheer me up, but she's doing the opposite.

Before getting back on my bike, I take out my phone to text Mari.

It's dead. No, not dead—off. I forgot I turned it off when I went into Gray's room. I power it back on.

Yikes! Two texts and three calls from my mother.

Where are you? the last text reads.

I think of calling her to tell her about Mrs. Wagner, but I decide I want to see her face when I share that. So I text a check-in instead.

> Me: Sorry, sorry!! My phone was off. Coming home right now.
>
> Mom: Where are you?
>
> Me: The Anchorage. I'll tell you everything when I get home.
>
> Me: Oh, and no need to go to the hospital if you haven't already. I got your wrap. 🖤☺️😊

"Better not go in there," says Calla when I'm barely off my bike. She and Joey are sitting on the front steps, trying to scrape silt from the mud flats off their boots with sticks.

"Mom's mad at me?"

"You can say that again," says Joey, who typically remains silent in times of family drama.

"Roses mad?"

"Worse," says Calla. *"Laundry mad."* Mom refuses to do that job in the summer when we're out of school, since we're the ones who have the time to get it done. "She received a call from Cecelia Hobbs."

"And?" Every second on the steps is one second longer that I'm not being chewed out by Mom.

"Apparently Cecelia heard that her cat—the one that died last year—was missing."

Omigod! Mrs. Wagner must have called Cecelia. Who knew they were friends? I sure didn't!

I head into the house, fairly certain that Mom will forgive me when she learns the reason for the lie.

"Sorry, Mom" I say, heading down to the laundry room. "But wait till you hear!"

"What were you thinking, Peyton?" she asks mid-fold. "Peeking in Mrs. Wagner's windows?"

"Her *garage* windows," I say. "That's not the same as looking into someone's house."

"Both are trespassing." Mom says, handing me one end of a fitted sheet. "And something tells me that you looked in other folks' windows, too!"

"I needed to help find the driver that hit Gray, and guess what? Mrs. Wagner's car wasn't in her garage. It's at the body shop!" I stop folding and hold the sheet close to my chest to better make my point. "Her car *needed body repairs*!"

Mom pulls the sheet away from me and finishes the last folds herself. "I know that. I already checked with Frank down at the body shop. He told me that Mrs. Wagner's car was there. She brings it in every June to get the winter dings out."

"From rocks and ice and stuff?"

She nods.

"What if he's covering for her?" I ask. "I mean, did you ask to see the car?"

"Peyton! I'm not law enforcement, and neither are you. Mrs. Wagner is our neighbor, and she was furious with your behavior. She thought I had put you up to it! Do you know how unethical that is? Not to mention embarrassing!"

"I was trying to help," I say. I want to tell her about the bike I found in the woods, to prove to her that I can be helpful, but I don't dare say more. "I didn't mean to embarrass you. I'll tell her it was all my idea."

Mom nods. "Yes, be sure to mention that when you apologize to her," she says.

My chest clenches. "May I write her a letter?"

"Nope," she says, putting a new load in the washer. "Now, would you like to tell me why you were at the hospital today when I expressly told you not to go there?"

When I can't come up with an immediate response, she closes the lid of the washer and sighs. "Come and sit down," she says.

Trust me, that's never a good thing to hear. The clenching in my chest grows tighter.

We move into the family room, and Bronwyn, who's practicing her lines for the community theater summer play, slides off the couch with a sigh and heads to her room.

While I slowly sit down next to Mom, my brain scrambles to get ahead of what she's going to say. "Mrs. Olsen said—"

"Peyton, I talked with your father this afternoon. We're worried about you. Mari's gone, and we think that Gray's accident is playing too big a part in your life. We know you're worried about him. We know that you'd like to see the driver brought to justice. But you are twelve, and this terrible incident should not be your summer obsession."

I flush. "It's not an obsession! How can you call

it that?" (Okay, maybe my *thoughts* have been obsessive, but it doesn't mean I'm *acting* that way!)

"We agreed that it would probably be best if you lived at the farm this summer. Dad and Grana need your help. Plus Aunt Beth is coming this week. She'd love to indulge her favorite niece."

Mom's making up this last part just to sweeten the decision. Aunt Beth doesn't have favorites.

Talk about quicksand! I feel like my whole world is disappearing right now.

I jump up. "This isn't fair," I yell. "You and Dad cannot keep doing this to us! I am not a houseplant that can be moved around depending on your needs!"

"It's not our needs we're thinking of! *You* need something more right now. How lucky you are, in some ways, to have two homes."

"Lucky for you, maybe!" I say, and tear up the stairs to my room.

Chapter 16

I don't speak at dinner. Not that anyone notices. Calla tells Mom that she should write an article on ocean acidification and how it has contributed to mussel depletion, and then Bronwyn tells a funny story about how her former boyfriend Finn fell off the stage during rehearsal and how Bronwyn tried to help him up but ended up pulling down a stage curtain.

"We're not going back there again, are we?" Mom says, meaning back to Finn. As Dad always says, Mom likes to cut to the chase.

"It would be *me* going back, not *us*," Bronwyn says defensively.

It would definitely be us, I want to say. *We'd all be caught up in the Finn drama again. Why isn't Bronwyn getting sent to the farm to keep her away from flirty Finn?* But I don't. Like I said, I'm not speaking.

As soon as the dishwasher's loaded and the countertops wiped off, I head to my room.

I have one goal right now, and that's to make sure I don't have to live at Bluff's Head this summer. Farming is not my ideal summer vision. My ideal summer vision is being with Gray. But as they say, a goal without a plan is just a wish.

And so I get busy planning.

I pull out the same notebook I used for my investigative work and stretch out, tummy down, on my bed. I figure my very best tack is to get a job in town, one that would keep me sufficiently busy. The desk clerk at the Anchorage told me to talk to the manager tomorrow, so perhaps that door isn't totally closed. That's my number-one priority. And if that doesn't work, maybe I can get someone else to hire me. I could walk dogs, babysit, or mow lawns.

I start a list of jobs and write down prospective employers. But as I'm trying to think of names, I realize that my chance of getting one of these odd jobs before Mom banishes me to the farm is just as unlikely—if not more unlikely—than getting a job at the Anchorage. Everyone around here knows that you have to get a jump on hiring summer help. People probably hired their sitters, walkers, and mowers back in May.

That realization makes me want to buckle down on the Anchorage job even more. Tomorrow I'll go to the hotel and plead with the manager if I have to. I list all the persuasive reasons he should hire me:

1. I'm an extremely focused worker.
2. I won't have a close friend working there this summer, so I won't get distracted from my duties (though see number one).
3. My mom and my sister worked at the Anchorage and loved it. I've always assumed it was my destiny, too.

I'm thinking that number three might be my strongest point. It has the human-interest angle, as Mom would call it. But what if the manager tells me to come back next year? I add:

4. If I'm not the fastest towel folder and politest water pitcher girl he's ever hired, he can fire me.

That last one seems pretty irresistible to me.

And once I have the job, I can tell Mom that I will be fully engaged in an activity that she herself inspired. I draw a smiley-faced Mom.

I need to make sure she doesn't ship me off to the farm tomorrow, though. I know—I'll tell her that I want to stay home one more day to apologize to Mrs. Wagner in person and to pack. That will be hard to argue with and should give me enough time to sneak down to the Anchorage.

My phone dings with a text from Mari.

*A guy gives his girlfriend a dozen roses and says,
"I will love you until these die."
She starts to panic until she realizes:
one of them is silk.*

    Me: OMG! ❤️❤️❤️❤️
    Mari: Saw it on Instagram. Sweet, huh?
    Me: Adding "be romantic" to my boyfriend list.

And I do. I take out my list and cross off *Love Narnia* and make number eleven *Be romantic* instead.

    Mari: Got my first kiss last night!
    Me: What?? And you didn't text me immediately?!???? What kind of best friend are you?

No response.

    Me: Tell me details! How many things does he check off on your boyfriend list?

Still no response.

I can't believe Mari got her first kiss! And I can't believe she didn't tell me about it right away. Come to think of it, we've barely texted since she left. I assumed she was busy watching the twins. But maybe she's been busy hanging out with Jared. I should be happy for her, I know, but I can't help thinking that she's living the summer of our dreams while I'm stuck here, trying to avoid sinking into quicksand.

I wait ten minutes for a response before finally giving up.

Enough waiting. To lower tensions with Mom and up the chances of my plan succeeding, I leave my room and break my vow of silence to apologize one more time, telling Mom that I will make a return visit to Mrs. Wagner's in the morning.

She's listening to the police scanner.

I hear that someone has been apprehended, and I can't stop myself. I ask if it's the hit-and-run driver.

If she is surprised by my speaking or thinks my question is out of line, she doesn't let on. "The state police have moved on to a bigger case."

Bigger than finding a potential killer? I want to shout, but I don't. It would show too much passion.

"Bigger?"

"The murder of a family up north."

Oh, okay. Bigger. But now I absolutely know that I have to be the one to make sure justice is done for Gray.

— ❤ —

I'm nervous as I ride my bike into town the next morning. Even though Mom said she'd be at a save-the-trees protest outside the state house in Augusta, she's known for changing her plans. She could just as easily get a lead on a new story and rush home to do research.

I pedal faster. Maybe I should head to Mrs. Wagner's right away, like I promised. But if I don't get this job at the Anchorage, my entire summer will be *over*. I'll go to Mrs. Wagner's just as soon as this task is completed.

I park my bike outside the Anchorage, straighten my nicest skort and blouse, and head inside.

There's a different desk clerk this morning. She's redoing her ponytail. I tell her that my name is Peyton Campbell and that I've come to speak to the manager. I feel more confident today, more determined.

"Are you here for a junior host job?" she asks with a slight French accent.

I nod.

"I'm sorry, but they're all filled."

I don't hesitate this time. "The clerk on duty yesterday suggested I return this morning and speak to Mr. K myself." I'm proud of how professional I sound.

The clerk bites her lower lip. I'm guessing that she's been told what to do and doesn't want to seem like she's being pushed around by a twelve-year-old.

I wait.

"Can you tell me which clerk told you to return?" she asks.

I could describe her, but I don't want to get her in trouble. She was at least trying to be helpful. Then it occurs to me that the manager might remember my mother. "You can tell the manager that I'm Tally Walsh's daughter."

She nods as if I've finally given her something she can work with.

"Mr. Kataski," she says, rapping softly on the door behind her before opening it a crack. "There is a young girl here to see you. She says she is Tally Walsh's daughter."

After a few moments, a man emerges. He's younger than I thought he would be, about my mom's age (so obviously he didn't hire her). I'm pretty sure I recognize him from the farmers market and maybe even from school events. I wonder if he has a kid my age.

"What can I do for you, miss?" he asks.

I tell him I'd like to work as a junior host. I tell him that I'm focused, hardworking, and—

"Didn't Ms. Ellis tell you that we have filled all our positions?" He looks up at the desk clerk and then back down at me.

"She did," I say, "but I need this job, and I promise I will be the best—"

He holds up his hand. "You know," he says, "you are a lot like your mother."

"You know my mother?"

He nods. "She occasionally fishes here for celebrity interviews. Always wants to know who of notoriety might be staying with us. And she is very persistent."

I cringe. Mom hates doing those interviews for *The Notes*, but it's a necessary part of her job. "Well, I might have her persistence, but I don't share her interest in celebrities," I say. "So, are you willing to give me a try?" I hope I'm mixing my mother's gumption with some of Bronwyn's persuasive charm.

He sighs. Then he half smiles.

I did it, I think! I solved the problem of my summer!

"I'm sorry," he says, shaking his head. "I'm sure you'd be one of the best. But I have already said no to several other kids. If word got out that I hired someone after turning away other deserving kids . . . well, that just wouldn't be good for business."

All the air seeps out of me. I'm not going to get the job I wanted, and it's my fault. If only I'd been prompter! I've been putting off asking for this position ever since I learned that Mari wasn't going to be here to do it with me.

"Thank you for talking with me, Mr. Kataski," I say, and head toward the doors.

If this were a movie, I'd reach the exit and hear, "Wait, kid!"

But this isn't a movie, and I'm out of luck. I can't believe I'm going to be working in the fields this summer instead of spending time with Gray.

I feel like screaming. How could I have been so stupid? "Never put off till tomorrow what you can do today"—hasn't Grana been telling me that for as long as I can remember? What I wouldn't give for a do-over.

I pull my bike out of the rack and ready myself for the dreaded ride out to Mrs. Wagner's.

But then I think of Gray. How could I leave without saying goodbye when I promised I'd never leave him?

So I head to the hospital one last time.

But wouldn't you know it, just as I'm turning onto Main Street, I see my mother striding down the other side of the street. Even though she's still at a distance, there's no mistaking her determined walk, her arms swinging high.

Without hesitation, I veer right, into a driveway, and duck behind a real estate office.

My heart pounds wildly (can twelve-year-olds have aneurisms?) as I wait to see if she continues down the street or crosses to confront me. Never mind my summer—my whole life will be over then.

She keeps walking.

Chapter 17

My presence at the hospital has become as regular as Grana's advice. I smile at the nurses as I pass the station and head back to Gray's room. Most of them know my name by now.

When I look in the window, I see that Mrs. Olsen is working. She's got a pile of file folders on the chair I've come to think of as mine, and she's reading something on her laptop.

Just as I'm wondering if I should knock, she lifts her head and waves me in.

"How is he?" I ask, standing on the other side of her, close to Gray's shoulders.

She shrugs. "I spent the early morning hours telling him stories, and I swear I could see micromovements in his face, but the doctor couldn't reproduce them. Apparently coma patients have involuntary reactions that have nothing to do with what's going on in the room."

"It doesn't mean they're waking up?"

She shakes her head.

I can tell she feels like crying, and I'm not sure what to do. If she were my mom, I'd wrap my arms around her shoulders.

She takes a deep breath. "They say that if a patient doesn't come out of a coma within the first couple of weeks, their chances of ever doing so drop considerably."

I quickly do the math. It's been six days.

Mrs. Olsen continues, "I'm sorry. Maybe I shouldn't have told you that. But I'm not giving up hope. Not one bit!"

"I'm not, either!" I say. "I'm glad you told me." I want her to know that I can handle all possibilities, even the worst.

And then I realize that it doesn't matter if I can handle the worst possibility or not. This might be the last time I see Gray Olsen. My head drops.

"I've upset you, haven't I?" She places her arm around my waist.

"It's not that," I assure her. "It's just that I probably won't get a chance to visit again. I have to work with my dad and grandmother on their farm, which is on the other side of the bay. Too far to come by the hospital on my bike."

"And you don't want to do that—work at the farm?"

"I like coming to the hospital. I like seeing Gray and being helpful." *Being a comfort*, I want to add, but don't. "I was so happy when you asked me to get your tea yesterday."

She nods, and it occurs to me that Mrs. Olsen is one of the nicest people I have ever met. She doesn't treat me like a pesky kid. She understands my concerns and talks to me like I have a perfect right to be thinking about Gray. (Which I do!) If Gray is even half as nice as his mom, well, he definitely checks off item number four!

"Here," she says, lifting up her file folders. "Come sit down."

I hate to give up my position so close to Gray's heart, but I walk around her and slide into the chair.

"What if I gave you a job?" she asks.

I sit up tall. "Like what?"

"What if I hired you to spend time with Gray a couple of hours a day? I've been relieved of my trial cases, but I still have to help prepare the lawyers who are taking over for me, and I can't make phone calls in here." Gray's mom is a lawyer? How did I not know that? "You could tell him the stories from the photo book that you've heard me tell. And you could describe his Halloween costumes and the gifts he got on his birthdays—that sort of thing."

Omigod! Coolest. Job. *Ever!* Wait till I tell Mari!

"I'd feel so much better knowing someone was here. I'll pay you, of course. And it doesn't have to be every day. His father will be here on weekends."

"I would love to!" I say.

"You'll have to clear it with your parents, of course."

Right. I wonder how that's going to fly. If they think I'm obsessed now, what will they think when they learn that I'm going to be spending a few hours a day with Gray?

Mrs. Olsen reaches down for her purse. "Here's my business card," she says. "Have your parents call me if they have any questions or concerns."

I look down:

Kathryn Olsen
Attorney-at-Law

How could they argue with this? (Well, okay. Maybe they'll argue some. But Mrs. Olsen obviously thinks it's healthy for me to be doing this.)

I stay and chat for a few minutes more, but then I explain that I have to cut my visit short today because I promised my mom I'd do something important. "Would you like me to start tomorrow?" I ask.

"Assuming it's all right with your parents, how about ten to noon tomorrow, and we'll see how it goes. You might find that it's more boring and difficult than you expect."

"Oh, no!" I say. "It's the perfect job!"

I take a last look at Gray, the beautiful boy. I study his face, wondering if he heard about the arrangement and hoping he's as happy about it as I am.

I don't bother to wait for the elevator and am practically skipping out of the hospital when I see Kayak Boy—who isn't Kayak Boy—talking with Ahmed at the information desk. What is he doing back at the hospital?

"How is he?" I hear him ask. "Do they think he'll wake up?"

He's asking about Gray! I pick up speed. "Hey!" I call to him. He looks up. "I thought you didn't know—"

"Thanks, Ahmed," he says, then turns and races toward the exit.

I consider chasing after him but decide my chances of getting information right here are higher.

"Peyton!" Ahmed says, his schoolwork spread out in front of him. "How are you doing, little one?"

"Not so little!" I say impatiently. "Who is that kid? Do you know him?"

Ahmed hesitates. "I believe his name is Jax."

"Jax? Is that short for something, like Jackson?"

"I couldn't tell you. He introduced himself as Jax."

"What's his last name?"

"That I couldn't tell you, either."

"What was he doing here?"

Ahmed points to the sign above his head. "Getting information."

"About Gray?"

"Sorry, little one. All inquiries at the information desk are confidential."

"Ahmed!"

"Why are you so curious? Even if he were asking about Gray Olsen, is it your job to screen all inquiries about him?"

I give him a big sigh. Clearly this conversation is getting me nowhere.

I say goodbye to Ahmed and head out the door just in time to see not–Kayak Boy—or *Jax*, I guess—jogging toward the back parking lot. Is he heading to his car—maybe one with a smashed-up front end, which is why he parked it around back—or did he walk here?

I turn around and head back into the hospital. Ahmed has gone back to his studies, but I stand in front of him until he raises his head.

"How are you doing, little one?" he asks with a totally straight face.

"Not so little," I say more patiently, knowing that this is the perfect opening for my question. "I'm almost thirteen now, you know. Say . . . how old do you think that Jax kid is?"

Ahmed's eyes smile like he's in on a big secret.

"I don't know," he says. "About your age, I'd guess. Maybe a little older. Why do you ask?"

The way he says that makes it clear he thinks he knows why I'm asking. "Absolutely not!" I practically shout. "It's not like that." I wait for the smile to disappear from Ahmed's face. "I just mean . . . do you think he could be sixteen?" In other words, is he old enough to have his license?

Ahmed frowns. "I'd be surprised if he was that old. But if so, he's definitely too old for you."

I don't bother telling him that I would *never* be interested in Jax. My mind is too full of more pressing thoughts. "Thanks for the information, Ahmed," I say, and take off.

I retrieve my bike and take a long gulp of water (*Motivate, Hydrate, Feel Great*) and realize that even though I'm on my way to see Mrs. Wagner, I do feel pretty great. Not only do I have a job that will keep me in town—and so close to Gray!—I also have a new lead on the hit-and-run driver.

Because really, who else would make a point of stopping by the hospital and inquiring about Gray (whom he supposedly doesn't even know)? It's a pretty short list: a reporter, like my mother; the officers on the case; Mr. Blake, the camp director; and me, the girl who found him. And the person who feels guilty for hitting him.

All I have to do now, I tell myself, is apologize to Mrs. Wagner.

When I pedal around the bend, Mrs. Wagner is sitting in a rocking chair on her front porch, like she's waiting for me. She has the same coffee mug as yesterday in hand.

I slide off my bike and walk it up her stone path.

She doesn't say hello or anything.

My earlier confidence evaporates. My body is suddenly shaky. "I'm sorry, Mrs. Wagner," I say as soon as I'm within earshot.

She leans forward ever so slightly. "Sorry for what, Miss Campbell?"

I come a little closer. "I'm sorry for trespassing, and peeking in your garage windows, and lying about the cat." I hope I've covered everything.

Still she waits.

So I add, "I want you to know that my mother had nothing to do with my snooping. She had no idea what I was up to, and she was pretty mad when she found out."

"You were convinced I was the one who hit that boy, weren't you? That I hit him and just drove off and left him to die."

It all sounds perfectly awful coming from Mrs. Wagner's mouth.

I think of lying, of telling her that I didn't think

any of those things, but then I'd have one more wrong piled on my conscience, so I nod. "I guess I don't know how someone would act when they're really, really scared of a horrible mistake they made."

Mrs. Wagner lifts her chin, then rocks back. "How are you acting now?"

I try to think, but my brain feels frozen. Am I doing the right thing?

I came here.

I said I was sorry.

I told the truth.

"Now you know," she adds.

"Know what, Mrs. Wagner?"

"What to do when you make a really horrible mistake."

Maybe that was her way of telling me I'd done the right thing, I think as I turn to head home. But it doesn't matter, because I will never allow myself to make another mistake again.

Ever.

Chapter 18

We've barely begun to eat dinner when Mom asks, "Did you apologize to Mrs. Wagner?"

"I did," I tell her, and take a sip of water to help the bit of brussels sprout that's stuck in my throat go down. "And I assured her that you didn't know about my snooping—that you had nothing to do with it at all."

"Thank you for that," she says. "I hope you have learned—"

"I got a summer job today!" I let slip. I really wanted to tell my mother about Mrs. Olsen's offer after dinner, when I might be able to get her alone, but the urge to change the subject is just too great.

Mom looks at me suspiciously over her raised fork. As far as she's concerned, I already had a summer job.

Both my sisters stop chewing to hear my answer.

"Mrs. Olsen offered me a job."

Mom lets her fork drop. She leans back in her

chair and gives me the Mom glare. I'm sitting across from her, so it's a direct hit.

"I didn't ask her to! I went to say goodbye, since I wouldn't be seeing them anymore. It seemed like the right thing to do."

Mom's still staring at me, but the corner of her mouth turns up a little, which is a very good sign. "And Mrs. Olsen just happened to offer you a job?"

"She needs to work a couple of hours a day, and she can't stand the thought of Gray not having someone beside him, talking to him, telling him stories."

"Doesn't Gray have other family?" Calla asks, talking with her mouth full.

"His father comes on weekends." But Calla has me thinking. There are lots of people in his photo album—aunts, uncles, cousins, and grandparents (though one grandfather is dead). Why haven't they come to visit him?

"His extended family lives in Norway," Mom says. "The Olsens have dual citizenship."

Cool! That's something I'll definitely want to ask him about when he's awake.

"You and your research," Bronwyn says to Mom.

I lean forward in my chair. "Um, what else have you learned?"

"Nothing pertinent to this discussion," Mom says, turning her attention back to me. "You know how I—how your father and I feel. We don't think it's healthy for you to spend so much time at the hospital."

I have to convince her. "It's not like I can just turn my concern off," I say. "If I'm at the farm, I'll still be worrying about Gray all the time. Only I won't be able to see for myself how he's doing." Plus I promised that if he hung on, I wouldn't leave him—and I won't. "This is something I can do with my concern, something positive."

Her face registers a crack—a moment of consideration.

"Unlike looking for banged-up vehicles," I add, "which wasn't at all productive."

Bronwyn helps herself to another veggie taco. "You know, Mom, you always tell us that real caring involves action. Peyton has found a way to act on her empathy."

Mom takes a sip of her wine and sighs. I can tell that she's wondering what my father and Grana will say. That's the problem with this family: too many adults to convince. And they all want an equal voice.

Truthfully it's Grana I worry about most. She's definitely going to have an opinion, and I don't think it's going to be one I'll like.

Sometimes I think it was Grana Mom divorced.

Mom leans forward. "You're right, Peyton," she

says. "Keeping you at the farm is not going to protect you from difficult truths. And, Bronwyn, you're right as well. Peyton is acting on her convictions."

"Am I right, too, Mom?" Calla asks, grinning.

"Of course, darling, you're always right," Mom says.

I groan along with Bronwyn as I get up and give my mom a hug. "I promise I'll keep my whims in check."

She gives me a smile, but I'm not sure she believes me.

I help clear the table and then retreat to my room. I start to text Mari, but I have too much to say, so I video call. She answers, but she's with Jared and several other kids. They're headed to an arts festival. I've barely told her my news when Mari tells the others that I have a new job babysitting a kid in a coma. *"What?"* one kid says. There are some giggles. I want to correct her, to say that it will be so much more than babysitting—that I've sort of been given a second chance to save his life—but she says she has to go.

"I'll call you back tomorrow," she says.

It's strange seeing Mari with new friends. She seems so relaxed and happy. It's as if she's having an even better summer than the one we planned. The call leaves me feeling hollow.

But then I remember that I, too, am having an extraordinary summer and that I have a job to do. So I move on to some research of my own. Granted, I don't have much to go on, but I do a search for the name Jax (also Jackson) and Mussel Cove, Maine. If he's a local a grade or two ahead of me, he might show up on a Little League roster or in an article about kids fundraising or something like that, and then I could learn his last name. If he's a summer kid, he might be on the yacht club's sailing list or something.

But there's nothing. Not even a social media account. Who isn't discoverable in this day and age?

I decide to do some research on hit-and-run accidents instead. I'm curious to learn more about how these cases are solved. From what I can tell, most drivers are found because of eyewitnesses (who either saw the accident itself or saw the car fleeing the scene) or the existence of debris. But I read about one driver who was caught because she kept calling the hospital to see if the victim was okay! Isn't that exactly what Jax is doing? Isn't he revealing his guilt every time he shows up there? I'm sure of it.

I'm tempted to race into the other room and tell Mom. After all, this could be the break she's looking for. But the timing isn't good. She barely agreed to my accepting the job with Gray. And I promised to keep my whims in check.

I recall a quote on my wall: "Knowledge is knowing what to say. Wisdom is knowing when to say it."

I'll try to get one more sighting, I think, to make the case rock solid. One more instance where Jax's curiosity about Gray is just too great for him to ignore.

Chapter 19

The next morning, I pull myself out of bed, eat some granola, and then—partly to show Mom (who has already left the house) that she made the right decision by letting me stay in town this summer and partly to make the time pass more quickly—I put on her gardening gloves and pick up the rose limbs scattered all around our back deck. The grass is wet from dew, and I keep brushing at my ankles, not knowing if it's grass sticking to my skin or hungry mosquitos. I've made my third trip to the compost pile when Bronwyn comes out on the back deck. She's got her tea, and I can smell the maple syrup.

"You're up early," I say.

She raises her eyebrows as if to say, *It ain't easy*.

"So, you're going into the hospital this morning, right?" she asks, sitting down on the only lounge chair. She stretches her legs out to catch some morning sun. "I think it's kind of cool that you'll be sitting with, uh—"

"Gray," I remind her, my insides feeling tickly. I can't help smiling.

She returns my smile. "Kind of romantic, huh?" Even Bronwyn seems to think we're destined to be together! "Well, if you're not with Gray this afternoon, I was wondering if you'd like to go Smokey's with me."

Smokey's Greater Shows is the carnival that comes to the fields on the edge of town every Fourth of July. But why is she asking me to go with her? Ever since she started high school, she's gone with friends after the fireworks. I'd been thinking of texting Lilliam to see if I could join her and Jamie.

"Did Mom ask you to take me?" I ask.

"Nope," says Bronwyn. "It was all my idea."

"Okay," I say. Maybe helping her little sister out last night felt so good that she wants to do it some more.

When I arrive at the hospital, Mrs. Olsen is leaning over Gray, running her fingers through his hair. She doesn't see me for a few moments, and I don't knock or wave or enter the room. Instead, I stand like a statue, practically holding my breath. It isn't until she sits down that I unfreeze and act as if I've just arrived.

I'm so nervous when I enter the room, knowing that Gray and I are going to be alone together for two whole hours. I've been practicing telling some of the stories I heard Mrs. Olsen share, but I still hope I can find enough to say to fill the time.

"Peyton," Mrs. Olsen says when I enter. "I forgot that today is the Fourth of July. You probably want to be out and about, watching the parade and hanging out with your friends."

I shake my head. "I'd rather be with Gray," I say. "The parade is really boring—mostly a bunch of old men in convertibles, Miss Mussel Cove, and a gazillion little kids on bikes. My sister Calla used to march with the middle-school band, but she swapped the clarinet for the mandolin, so no need to cheer her on today."

She laughs. "Well, thank you for being here." She gets up and gathers her things. "It may be a holiday, but I'm happy for the time to catch up. I'll be back around noon."

"See you soon!" I say, and pick up the photo book she left on her chair.

"Oh," she says, coming back into the room, "there's a button here." She shows me how it's on the end of a cord on the side of Gray's bed. "Press this if you need to call a nurse. They're typically in and out, but today has been so calm. There must be fewer nurses on duty. If you see anything that concerns you, don't hesitate to ring one of them."

"I won't," I say as reassuringly as I can. I watch her leave the room, then slide into her chair.

"Hi, Gray. It's Peyton."

I study his face, but it shows no reaction. Seven days.

I glance up at the monitor and am happy to see that the lines are blipping up and down in the normal way—or the normal way for someone in a coma, that is.

I lean closer to Gray and clear my throat. "Your mom asked me to hang out with you while she catches up on work. I've got your photo book on my lap, and I'm going to remind you of things that happened in your life, just like she does. Okay?"

I find one of my favorite pictures—one of him on his fifth birthday. He's dressed like a dinosaur, and it looks like he's chasing some kids in his backyard. I remind him of the year he was a *Tyrannosaurus rex* and how his aunt made him a costume that had long claws and everything. "Your cake was a dinosaur, too. It looks really impressive! I wonder if it was made by a bakery. I bet it's a chocolate cake. That's my favorite, too!"

I try to remember my fifth birthday party but can't. "I remember my seventh birthday," I tell Gray. "My grandmother thought it would be fun to have a tea party theme. She put out a lace tablecloth and her best china teacups and plates. Then she served us miniature sandwiches and tiny bite-size sweets. My friends from school couldn't care less about a tea party. They got up from the table and began marching around, saying, 'We're not ladylike!' My grandmother was appalled, but my mother thought it was the funniest thing she'd ever seen. I just sat at the table so I wouldn't hurt my grandmother's feelings."

I turn a few more pages, retelling the stories that I've heard Mrs. Olsen tell. Every now and then, I glance up at the clock to see how much time I have left. I'm not in a hurry to leave, but Mrs. Olsen is right; it's not as easy to fill two hours as I thought it would be.

When I have a half hour left, I decide to peek ahead in the book. I want to see more recent pictures of Gray.

I turn to the end of the album. There's a group selfie of Gray and his parents sitting at a table in what seems to be an ice cream shop. Gray is in the middle, a huge ice cream sundae in front of him. It's easy to imagine their laughter as they try to huddle close enough to fit in the picture.

I feel a little throb between my eyes. I have ten years of photographs in the "Peyton Album" of my family posing together, smiling in an easy, familiar way. And then those photos stop. Sure, Mom and Dad still pose on either side of me at special events, like my sixth-grade graduation. But even though we're standing in the very same spots we might have stood in before the divorce, the pictures feel more ghostly. Like they're pictures of what's not instead of what is. Weird, I know.

"You're still a family, Peyton," Mari said once, "even if your parents aren't married." It was a very comforting thing for her to say.

I look up at Gray and just know he'd be equally reassuring.

I turn the page.

There's a caption at the top of this page: SPRING FLING. There are several pictures of boys and girls all dressed up, and the party appears to be at a lodge—or maybe a country club? Definitely somewhere fancy.

And then I see it.

It's a picture of Gray standing next to a girl in front of some lilac bushes. She's got long dark hair and is wearing a sleeveless flowered dress with a flouncy skirt. Was she his date?

Does Gray have a girlfriend?

I scrutinize the picture. He isn't holding her hand or even touching her. In fact, they look like they're uncomfortable posing together. Maybe they're cousins?

Then I remember what Mom said about his

extended family being in Norway. Not cousins, then. But that doesn't mean they're *together*.

For some reason, I have the sudden urge to get up and retrieve my boyfriend list from my backpack. I glance at all of the items Gray has checked off. And I think of all that Gray and I have been through together.

The girl in the picture isn't here now. She didn't find Gray in the road, and she isn't trying to help him regain consciousness.

I tuck my boyfriend list into my pocket and come back to Gray. Being careful not to disrupt any of the wires that surround the bed, I reach out with my pointer finger and gently touch his hand. It's warm.

"Gray," I say, and somehow I know that he's listening. "I think I know who might've done this to you—and I'm going to prove it. I promise."

Chapter 20

Bronwyn borrows Mom's car to take Calla and Joey and me to Smokey's. The song "Try, Try, Try" comes on the radio, and it makes me think of Mari. I wonder when she's going to call. I pull out my phone and send her a video of Bronwyn and me belting out a verse. I especially love my sister in this moment.

The rides are in a field on one side of the road, and parking is in the field on the other side. No sooner is the car in place than Calla and Joey peel off. They're not nearly as interested in the rides as they are in the animal competitions. The rabbit race is in five minutes.

Bronwyn and I buy our entry bracelets and begin walking down the midway, where accordion music competes with roller coaster screams. "Win a prize every time!" a man in front of a dart game calls into the crowd. The smell of cinnamon from the fried dough vendor makes me hungry.

I expect my sister to ask me what I want to ride

first, but she's distracted, clearly trying to figure out if there's anyone here she knows. I don't mind. It gives me a chance to scan the crowd, too. There's someone specific I'm hoping to find. And when I do find him, I'm going to ask a whole list of questions. Like: *How old are you? Do you have your license?* And *Why do you keep checking on Gray Olsen if you supposedly don't even know him?*

While I don't know for sure that Jax will be here, the odds are good: all of Mussel Cove comes to the carnival on the Fourth of July. And besides, with all the times I've crashed into him, I'm beginning to believe that solving this crime is my destiny, too.

Based on his performance at the farmers market, I'm guessing he'd be drawn to activities where you can show off. The games, probably. Or maybe he's an even bigger braggart, competing in the chain saw competition or trying to ring a bell by wielding a sledgehammer. I keep my eyes open for those grandstands.

Suddenly Bronwyn grabs my arm and pulls me through the throng toward the kiddie rides—way at the back of the field. It isn't until we reach the low-flying elephants that she slows down.

What the—?

"Finn!" she calls.

Finn?

He's sitting on a bench next to the kiddie car merry-go-round. Toddlers are sitting in trucks, planes, cars, and buses and are all steering madly, convinced they are the ones propelling these mini machines.

"Bronwyn!" Finn says, jumping off the bench.

"Hey," she says. "I didn't expect to see anyone at this time of day! You know Peyton, right?"

"'Course I do!" Finn says, like he and I used to hang out together all the time. Truth is, he hardly ever talked to me when he was at the house. He and Bronwyn would turn on a movie for all of us, then go make out in the laundry room.

"What are you doing way back here?" Bronwyn asks, motioning to the kiddie rides around us.

"My cousins are here from Massachusetts. They're two and four. I'm in charge of them today while the adults climb Ragged Mountain."

"*Really?*" Something in Bronwyn's tone makes me suspicious. Did she really have no idea that Finn would be babysitting at Smokey's today? "Which ones are your cousins?"

Finn points to two kids, an older boy and a younger girl, sitting together in a motorboat. Each has a steering wheel, but the two-year-old keeps pulling her brother's hands off his. Clearly she's got a destination in mind.

And just like that, I can see where this rendezvous

is going. We are moments away from Bronwyn suggesting that I watch the little kids while she and Finn run off to ride the Zipper together.

"Look what I have!" a girl calls.

We look up to see Lyndsay, one of Bronwyn's best buds, approaching. She's dyed her hair silver, which looks really cool, and is holding a candied apple in each hand.

"Bronwyn!" Lyndsay says.

"You didn't tell me you were going to be here," Bronwyn says.

"Neither did you!" says Lyndsay. She hands Finn a candied apple and smiles at me. "Are you babysitting, too?" she asks Bronwyn.

Normally I'd bristle at this, but I feel so bad for my sister right now! Clearly Lyndsay and Finn are here together, and neither one bothered to tell Bronwyn. I give Bronwyn a tiny little nod in case she wants to go with the babysitting alibi.

"No, Peyton is perfectly capable of looking after herself," she says. "I just wanted to spend time with my little sister. Her best friend is out of town for the summer, and I know how hard it is to lose a good friend." She stares at Lyndsay, who retreats behind her apple.

As if on cue, the merry-go-round stops, and Finn hustles over to help his cousins get out of the boat.

But instead of getting off the carousel, they run to the next vehicle in front of them—a motorcycle. Some folks never tire of going around and around, I think.

Lyndsay starts to say something, but Bronwyn cuts her off. "Well, nice to bump into you guys!" she says. "We were just headed to the restrooms." She nods toward the edge of the field behind them. "The porta-potties way out here always have the shortest lines."

I'm impressed by how quickly Bronwyn can think on her feet, though I wonder if Lyndsay and Finn actually buy it. I try to think of something consoling to say as we stand in line for the toilets.

"Sometimes the thing we want is the last thing we need," I finally say.

She makes a sound between a snort and a cry. "Is that one of the quotes on your wall?"

"It's not a quote. It's just something I was thinking."

She looks at me then like I'm not her little sister. She looks at me like I'm her friend—a real friend, not a friend like Lyndsay.

"That's good!" she says. "And you're absolutely right. Sometimes the thing we want *is* the last thing we need! Finn and Lyndsay are both egotists . . . and devious! Let them have each other. Come on!"

She grabs my hand, and we race past the kiddie

area; I guess she no longer cares about her charade of visiting the porta-potties. "What ride do you want to go on?"

Truthfully it doesn't matter what we do as long as Bronwyn and I are laughing together.

But she's waiting for an answer, so I say, "Let's do the Ferris wheel first."

It's the perfect vantage point from which to scan the crowds for Jax.

I search the area below us as the Ferris wheel starts and stops until it's fully loaded. Bronwyn rocks our car when we're at the tippy-top, which would normally scare me, but today I hardly notice, I'm so intent on finding Jax before we leave.

And then I do.

Chapter 21

Jax is right in front of us, standing in line for the ball toss.

I'm out of my seat the moment the carnival worker lifts the metal bar, releasing us from our fake hot-air balloon.

"Where are you going?" Bronwyn shouts as I race away.

I turn back momentarily; there's no time to explain the whole thing. "There's someone I need to talk to. I'll meet you at the fried dough stand," I call.

There's a long line at the ball toss. Jax is only two people from the front. He's in shorts and flip-flops, and he's got his hands pressed together as he watches a big guy whip balls at a little metal plate. Hitting the plate will release the lever and dunk the clown into a pool of water below. The clown in his cage heckles, "You call that a throw? You couldn't hit a wall if you ran into one!" Jax taps his thumbs together as if he's building energy that's about to be sprung.

I start to see red as I think about Jax having fun at a carnival on the Fourth of July while Gray is trapped in a hospital bed and might never see a carnival again.

I want to march right up to him, but I don't want people to think I'm cutting in line.

Before I can make up my mind about what to do, a woman approaches Jax. "There you are!" she says. Behind her is the same older man I've seen a couple of times before. Jax's mother and grandfather, I'm guessing.

I pull out my phone, hoping to sneak a picture I can send to Mari. *Look!* I'll text her. *This is the kid who ran over Gray!* Heck, maybe it'll be the picture I show the police to identify the hit-and-run driver.

I wait until Jax's face is in view and take the picture. Mission accomplished! I stuff the phone back into my pocket just as Jax turns and sees me.

Our eyes lock. His are soft, sad eyes.

Then it seems to hit him who I am. He snaps his head forward, pretending he doesn't recognize me.

For some reason, this makes me furious. We both know he saw me! Does he really think he can hide from me in plain sight? Maybe he thinks I won't approach him with his family around. Well, he *clearly* doesn't know me!

I start to push my way toward him when his grandfather turns to the others in line and shouts, "So, you think you can dunk the chef, do you? Want to get me back for all that sauce on a shingle I served?" He turns and walks toward the dunk tank. "All right, then."

"Dad!" Jax's mom shouts at the same time Jax yells, "No, Gramps!"

Jax's mom tries to grab her father's arm, but he slips past her and starts climbing the ladder to the dunk tank.

"Hey, buddy," the clown says as Jax's grandfather reaches the top of the ladder and rattles the cage.

"Hey, Gramps!" Jax calls. "Watch me throw!" He has made it to the front of the line and grabs the first ball. Then he makes some really elaborate arm movement, like he's never thrown a ball in his life. Unsurprisingly the ball doesn't even come close to hitting the metal plate.

"Darn!" Jax says dramatically, like he's sure he was aiming perfectly. His grandfather stares at the ball with a blank expression.

What are these two playing at?

"Watch, Gramps!" Jax yells, and throws another wild ball. "Darn it!" he says, sounding so disappointed that I almost believe him.

"Jackson!" says his grandfather, his expression now focused. He starts down the ladder, his voice calm. "That's no way to throw a baseball. You gotta wind up the way I showed you." He walks toward his grandson, then takes the ball and models the proper way to throw.

Jax's mom smiles apologetically at the people in line behind them. "Come on, Dad," she says, taking his arm. "Let's get that sausage roll you wanted."

Jax watches his mother and grandfather walk away. Then he takes his third ball, winds up, and throws it with so much force that the metal plate gongs when it's hit. The unsuspecting clown splashes into the water. The crowd seems to hold its breath until he reemerges. Then there're cheers.

A perfect pitch.

"Hey, kid!" says the man handing out the baseballs. "You forgot your prize."

Jax ignores him. To avoid eye contact as he passes me, he bends down and pretends to pick something up from the ground.

I could still go after him, still confront him about Gray. But something about the scene that just unfolded makes me reluctant to do so.

No matter. I've got my prize. I pull my phone out to inspect the picture I took. It's good. And I bet Mari will say he's cute.

Which is the only thing I'll give him on my boyfriend list.

Chapter 22

We always watch the fireworks from *Silly Whim*. The tide is low tonight, though, which means our tidal shore has turned into mudflats, so Dad can't come and get us. Instead, Mom drives us to Bluff's Head and follows us up to the back porch. Dad, Grana, and Aunt Beth are hanging out in the rocking chairs.

Aunt Beth jumps into my mother's arms for a hug. They've always been close, and they've remained so even after the divorce. Grana, on the other hand, gets up and heads inside with barely a nod at my mom. Mom, Dad, and Aunt Beth talk about a friend they have in common, and then Mom and Aunt Beth make plans to see each other later in the week.

I used to think, in happy moments like this one, that there was a chance my parents would get back together. But when I said as much to Mom one time, she said, "Button, I never would have caused all that pain if I wasn't one hundred percent certain it was the right thing to do." Which just confused me more. I mean, how can something that causes so much pain be the right thing to do?

After some more talking, Mom tugs on Beth's braids, tells the rest of us to have fun, and then drives off. Usually her leaving makes me feel sad, but she casually mentioned on the way over that she has a date tonight, and that's something I don't want to think about at all. (If Dad has been on any dates, we haven't heard about it.)

The shore in front of Bluff's Head is considered "deep water," which means that even when the tide is low, there's enough water to get the boat off the dock. Grana hands us bags and coolers and blankets, and we trail down the hill, onto the pier, and down the gangway. Dad boards first, stows our gear, and then gives the okay for the rest of us to join him. I start to follow my sisters and Aunt Beth to the bow of the boat when Grana touches my shoulder. "Get caught up with your aunt, and then come help me in the stern."

Yikes. No doubt *help me* is code for *I want to talk to you about why you're not staying at the farm over the summer.*

"Okay, Grana," I say chirpily, trying to sound like everything's A-OK between us.

Normally Dad zips around the harbor a bit, but boats have already begun to anchor, and he wants to get a decent viewing spot. Being part of a bobbing fleet feels special. This is my favorite part of the holiday.

As soon as Dad cuts the engine, Aunt Beth asks Bronwyn, Calla, and me a gazillion questions about our school year and plans for the summer.

Bronwyn tells a story about prom at the Anchorage and how Finn and some of his friends got drunk and tried to dance with the ice sculpture. It's the first time I've heard this story. I don't think she would be telling it if she still wanted to get back together with Finn.

Aunt Beth laughs, and I wonder why she doesn't point out that none of those boys are twenty-one, which means they were breaking the law. Grana would have mentioned it, for sure.

The sunset makes our faces glow, and I pull out my phone to take a picture of my sisters with Aunt Beth.

"Get in here," Beth says. She takes a selfie using my phone. Then she wraps both her arms around my waist. "I heard that you've had a big adventure," she says.

Even though she's probably heard everything from Dad and Grana, she says she wants to hear it from me. So I tell it all again, leaving out the part about Mrs. Wagner and my suspicions about Jax.

Then Calla starts telling her about counting mussels and a music festival coming up where she's actually going to play a full set with a band, and I slip away to the stern, where Grana is pulling plates and napkins out of a Bean tote bag.

Might as well get this talk over with.

There's an open cooler at Grana's feet, and momentarily she'll turn it into a little table topped with our favorite boat snacks, like sardines on crackers and crab dip. I know there are some seven-layer bars in that cooler, too.

"Sit down next to me, Peyton," she says, handing me a box of crackers. "What's your mom doing tonight?"

I hate it when Grana fishes for information.

"She mentioned having plans, but I didn't ask her for details," I say, which is a way of answering that Bronwyn taught me. She said, "Answer the question without giving any specific information. That way, you can't be put in the middle." It's a good trick, but it makes me sad that we have to be so careful with our own family.

When I was little, Grana and I were nearly inseparable. I loved to hang out with her in the barn while she made floral arrangements. She'd tell me the meanings of all the flowers. I remember being jealous of Calla because she was named after a flower that means *magnificent beauty*. She said that my parents should have named me Camellia, which means *loyal in love*. "You are my sweet camellia," she'd say.

It's been a while since she called me that, and from the look on her face, she won't be saying it anytime soon. "I'll arrange these crackers on a plate," I say.

"I want you to know that I'm extremely disappointed with your decision to stay in town."

I should be better prepared for this, but I'm not. "I know, and I'm sorry. It's just that . . ." I start again: "I know that there are lots of ways I can help you on the farm, Grana," I say, "but none of them feel quite as necessary as helping Gray—the boy who was hit. If there's even a chance—however small—that by spending time with him, I could help him recover . . ."

I want my grandmother to look at me. I hate letting her down.

"I have to try, Grana."

She concentrates on refolding a napkin. "I just don't get it. I would have thought that being with your family—especially your daddy, who loves you very much—in the home you grew up in would feel right and necessary, too."

How to respond?

Her eyes lock on mine. "It was bad enough when you chose your mother over your father. Now you're choosing some strange boy—a boy in a coma, no less!"

A boat passes, and the wake rocks us.

I feel slapped.

I search desperately for something to say that will make things right.

Only you know how sometimes, when you're searching for the correct words, all the wrong, inappropriate words bubble to the top? Like: *Is Grana really thinking about what's best for me, or am I just a prize she's determined to win?*

As quickly as this thought comes, I squeeze it out.

I don't want to be anything but her sweet camellia.

I try to push the reset button (as Dad would suggest) and ask her a question.

"Grana," I say, nibbling on a broken cracker, "do you remember when we were at the farmers market, and there was this older man dancing? A kid, maybe his grandson, joined him?"

I can tell she's not happy with the change in subject. Not one bit. "This past Saturday?" she says, her voice littered with pins.

"Yeah, remember? Calla was playing, and you called the man a fool."

She pulls the tab back on a sardine can and winces. "Did I really say that?"

I nod.

She takes a deep breath and shakes her head. "Will McCallister. He's always been something of a character," she can't help telling me. "Wonderful chef, though. He was the caterer at Aunt Beth's party when she got her graduate degree. Why do you ask?"

"Just wondering," I say. "I saw him and the kid again at the hospital the other day."

She makes a sympathetic sound. "I hear he stopped cooking. Apparently he can't drive any longer."

This is just the sort of information I'd hoped Grana would have. "Does he live in town?"

She shakes her head. "Out on Old Post Road—at least, that's where he used to live. I delivered his check there."

Old Post Road is in the direction of Bluff's Head, but when you come to a major intersection, you drive away from the shore instead of heading toward it. There aren't many houses out there. There are a few farms and a lot of woods. My breath quickens. "So how's he getting around?" I ask, knowing full well how he's managing.

"Cecelia Hobbs," Grana says, opening a Moxie and handing it to me.

What? "Mrs. Hobbs?" I take the can, happy for the peace offering.

"I saw her at church. She's been taking him to the hospital for tests. They suspect Alzheimer's." Her face shows genuine concern.

Alzheimer's. That's so sad. "Does his grandson live with him?"

"Not normally. He and his mother live in Portland. Apparently it's the grandson's job to care for him this summer. The boy's too young, but his mother needs to keep her job to pay for his medical care. She comes up most weekends."

Pieces fall together: Mr. McCallister's behavior at the farmers market and the fair. Seeing Cecelia Hobbs in the gift store. Running into Jax at the hospital. I guess he really *wasn't* looking for Gray.

The awful feeling I got while standing in Mrs. Wagner's driveway washes over me again. Starting today, I will stop jumping to conclusions and condemning people I don't even know.

And then another awful feeling hits me. I promised Gray I'd help find the driver who hit him, and I don't have a single lead.

Chapter 23

Mari never called me back, I realize as Dad drives me to the hospital the next morning. I suppose being with new friends can make you forget about the old ones.

"Here you go, kiddo," Dad says as he pulls up to the main entrance.

"Do you want to come in?" I ask. "You could meet Mrs. Olsen."

I can tell by the drop in his shoulders and his retreat into his seat that the answer is going to be no. "I don't think so," he says. "I've got some folks I need to check in with here in town."

"Okay, Dad," I say, "See you tomorrow." (We'll be at Mom's tonight since Dad had us for the Fourth of July.)

"Right," says Dad. "Love you."

Both Mr. and Mrs. Olsen are sitting by Gray's side when I arrive. Mr. Olsen looks like he hasn't slept in weeks.

"We're very grateful to you, Peyton," he says

after Mrs. Olsen introduces us. "We have to talk to the neurologist and the physical therapist—it could take some time."

"But I got you these," Mrs. Olsen says, handing me a couple of teen magazines. "I saw them in the gift shop, and they made me smile. I used to read them when I was your age. I thought you might need to take breaks from talking."

"Thanks!" I say, but I don't think I will ever tire of talking to Gray. "Don't worry if it takes longer than two hours," I add. "I don't have to be anywhere this afternoon."

I wait until they leave the room, and then I slide into the seat closest to Gray's bed and look around. The sad thing about the rooms in the ICU is that they never change. Nothing new and cheery ever arrives, and so there's nothing that needs to be removed or tidied up. Even the dim light stays the same.

"Hi, Gray," I say, thinking that he *must* recognize my voice by now. "Could you hear the fireworks last night?" It's possible; the hospital isn't far from the dock where they're launched. "I could feel the explosions in my chest! Did you know it was the Fourth of July?"

Gray gives a little nod.

Omigod! Did he really do that? Did he nod?

It was probably an involuntary movement, I

remind myself. Mrs. Olsen told me about them. Even though it looked like Gray was nodding, the fact that he moved his head at the end of my question was probably just a coincidence.

But what if it *wasn't* random? I reach for the call button and hold it in my hand, watching. He doesn't move again.

"Did you hear the fireworks last night?" I ask.

No response.

"Did you know it was the Fourth of July?"

No response.

"Gray, can you hear me?"

Nothing.

I drop the button, glad I didn't call a nurse. I don't want to be like the boy who cried wolf.

I glance down at the magazines in my lap.

"Be Your Best Self: Three Steps to a Better You" one of the headlines reads. I can't wait to read that article. I've been working hard to perfect my character, but there's still so much room for improvement.

"You should see the wall in my room, Gray. It's filled with quotes—wise sayings that are like directions for a happy life. One of my favorites is 'A smile is a curve that sets things straight.' I know it sounds sort of corny, but it's true, isn't it? When you wake up, you'll see a million grins, I promise you."

I set the magazines aside and pick up Gray's photo

book. There's a stack of cards tucked into the back. It seems funny to send cards to someone in a coma, but I suppose people are being optimistic. They're expressing their hope that he'll wake up, sending all their good thoughts and prayers.

Despite the fact that they're mostly addressed to Gray, the envelopes have been opened. Maybe Mrs. Olsen reads the cards aloud to him. Maybe reminding Gray of all the people who love him and are rooting for him is part of his therapy, just like telling him his stories. Maybe, I think, opening one of the envelopes, I should do the same.

The first one I pull out is from a Norwegian cousin working at Disney World. He tells Gray that his parents—Aunt Nina and Uncle Fredrik—send their love and that he's looking forward to the day when they can play a rousing game of Risk again. It's signed *Barrett*.

"My parents used to play Risk with us, back before the divorce," I tell him, "but it always led to arguments. They can be very competitive."

The next just says, "We're sending all our love" and is signed *The Masons*. I look to see if Gray's face registers the message, but I can't detect a change.

The third card is from a kid—you can tell by the handwriting—and he or she has written a lot. I read the first two sentences silently.

Omigod!

It's from Kayak Boy—the real Kayak Boy! His name is Noah Easton. He writes:

> *Man, I can't tell you how many times I've wished we hadn't cooked up this race. If only we'd left an hour earlier, like you wanted to. You and I would have been sitting at Day's together, challenging each other to a donut-eating contest.*

For the first time, I wonder what he did when Gray didn't show up. How long did he wait? Did he hear about the accident while he was still in town, or was he just worrying about the time (and the consequences) as he paddled back to camp? Did the police bother to question him? Did Mom?

I picture the boys racing. Winding Lane wraps closely around the bay. Gray would have been able to see the kayak out on the water, would have been able to gauge his chances of winning. Was he looking out at the water when he was hit?

Noah probably couldn't see Gray on shore, though—not without binoculars. But he might have heard something. Sound travels easily across water. And there wouldn't have been many working boats in the harbor at that time. Did he hear the screeching of tires? Did Gray scream?

The thought makes me want to curl into a little ball. I peek at Gray's face and try to fathom the pain he might have experienced.

The last time I saw Gray, I told him I had likely found the guy who hit him. Now I feel like a fraud. I have nothing at all.

Noah's return address is on the envelope. I pull out my phone and take a picture. Maybe a conversation with the real kayak boy could help.

It's starting to rain as I leave the hospital, so I call home to see if Bronwyn can pick me up. Fortunately Mom's working at home, so the Honda is there. My sister tells me to wait under the awning out front.

On the way back through town, we stop at the IGA to pick up some groceries. I'm in the produce aisle, trying to see if the flowers are from Sea Spray (Dad has been trying for forever to convince them to carry our flowers) when I bump into L&J.

"Sorry I haven't called you guys," I say. "I've been working at the hospital."

"We know," Jamie says. "Mari told us."

"Mari?" *My* Mari? "What did she say?"

"That you're being your saintlike self and reading to the coma kid."

The *saintlike* part makes me happy. I mean, who doesn't want to feel like they're doing good in the world? But I kind of wish Mari had shared her romantic thoughts about Gray and me being destined to be together. I wonder if there's a way I can convey that idea—an idea that seems more real than ever now that I'm spending every day with him.

But before I can figure out what to say, Jamie sighs. "Mari is *so* lucky. I can't believe she found someone as over-the-top romantic as she is."

"I know!" Lilliam says. "Can you believe that locket Jared gave her?"

Locket? My head is swirling. How is it that L&J know about a locket that I've heard nothing about?

Jamie doesn't seem to notice that I'm having difficulty keeping up. "Meanwhile, we're left here in quaint little Mussel Cove, where it's nearly impossible to meet anyone new unless you can afford to join the yacht club."

"Mari was so smart to ask if she could live with her aunt for the summer," says Lilliam, sighing.

"Mari didn't want to go to Gloucester," I interject, pleased to know something they don't. "We were going to work at the Anchorage together."

Lilliam and Jamie share a look that tells me they're holding something back. I'm about to ask what it is, but then Bronwyn joins us with a tote bag of groceries, and I decide that maybe I don't want to know.

Chapter 24

Saturday morning pack-up. I put my investigative notebook in my backpack, determined to get in touch with Noah Easton while I'm at the farm.

I started to text Mari about the locket last night, but I couldn't find the words. I wanted to be excited for her (a gift from her first boyfriend!), but I was so hurt that L&J had heard the news first. But every time I tried to write *that*, I glanced at my previous text—the one in which I blasted her for not telling me about the first kiss as soon as it happened—and it looked like I was doing nothing but scolding.

But why *didn't* she tell me about her first kiss right away? And why didn't she tell me about the locket or call me back when she said she would? Are we best friends or not?

As I pack the book I'm reading along with my glasses case, I wonder if she misses me, misses picking out our fall wardrobes, misses filling out our boyfriend lists. Has she even used hers with Jared?

I reach into the bottom of the backpack to find my own boyfriend list. Mari may or may not be on the right path this summer, but I have a list that reassures me that I am. My fingers touch Gray's sunglasses, but I can't feel the paper. Not anywhere.

I dump out the things I've packed so far and feel around inside. My fingertips cover every inch of fabric. It's not there.

My list is gone.

Pants pocket! I remember putting it in my pants pocket when I was visiting Gray last. I check all my pants and shorts, even ones I know I haven't worn in the last two weeks. No list.

I go down and check the top of the dryer. There are coins and gum wrappers, a small pencil, and some hair elastics, but no folded paper.

It's weird—I feel kind of vulnerable without the list. Less sure of myself. I sit down on my floor, lean against my bed, and try to think of everywhere I've been. Where could I have dropped it? Gray's hospital room?

The thought of Mrs. Olsen picking it up and reading it mortifies me! Even if she didn't guess that I was thinking of Gray as boyfriend material, I wouldn't want her to know I'm thinking about this stuff at all, or that I need a *list* to be sure I choose the right person.

I pull out my phone and scroll through my pictures

to jog my memory. There's Noah's address. There are the ones of my sisters and Aunt Beth. (Omigod, please don't tell me that Dad or Grana found it on the boat deck. *Please*.)

There's the picture of Jax with his grandfather at the fair, which I never did text to Mari. My heart gives a little tug knowing that Jax is helping to care for him. It was only a little more than two years ago that my grandfather died. He was funny and hardly ever said a bad word about anyone. He was my mom's biggest cheerleader.

Omigod, I hate losing things! Even something as minor as this list. I mean, I know I can copy it over. It's not like I don't have the time, or that I don't have it memorized, or that it changes anything about my life, right? So why do I feel this way?

I glance over at Calla's side of the room. She hasn't even started to pack. So I put down my phone and pull out my markers and another sheet of identical stationery and write my boyfriend list again.

My new list looks great. I tuck it into my backpack, pull out my packing list, and begin getting ready for Dad's all over again.

Once I've completed my farm chores (no mention of my boyfriend list, phew!), I sneak up to my little room. The temperature's rising in here, and I need to ask Grana to help me set up a fan, but it's the one place where I can get cell reception and am guaranteed privacy. I grab my phone and begin searching for a Noah Easton in Waterbury, Connecticut. He comes up right away.

I DM him and tell him who I am and how I'm spending time with Gray. I tell him that I got his name from Mrs. Olsen (which is sort of true; she left the cards out for me to read) and that I'd love to ask him some questions, if he doesn't mind.

He answers immediately!

> Noah: Glad you messaged me! No one is telling me anything! How is Gray? Do they think he's going to wake up?
> Me: They're hopeful. He sometimes moves, but supposedly the movements don't mean anything. Still, I can't help feeling that he's in there, listening to everything we say to him.
> Noah: Ask me anything. I can't believe they haven't found the driver yet!

I start by asking him to tell me everything he remembers about that morning. He tells me that he may have heard the accident while paddling. He heard a thump but assumed it was a car going over a bump. (Not an unreasonable assumption; our road has lots of potholes.) He stayed at Day's as long as he could, but then he panicked. He thought Gray might have tricked him into leaving camp and buying donuts, that it was all a big joke—that would be just like Gray, he'd said. He hustled back and learned the news soon after. He was questioned by the police, but he didn't have anything useful to tell them.

I ask him if he noticed anyone acting strange while he was in town. (I am, after all, the daughter of an investigative reporter.)

> Noah: Strange how?
>
> Me: Distressed. Worried.
>
> Noah: I don't think so.
>
> Me: OK. ☹
>
> Noah: There was an old lady who was having trouble ordering her donuts. She couldn't decide what she wanted and had to keep starting over. Haha!
>
> Me: That could be half our town. ☺ Thanks for all these answers.
>
> Noah: Thanks for being in touch. Let me know how Gray is doing. I feel so crappy about everything.
>
> Me: Hey! Not your fault.

(Then I remember the way I blamed Jax when I thought he was Kayak Boy, and I feel my own wave of guilt.)

> Noah: Hope you find the driver.
>
> Me: Me too.

I put my phone down and record his answers in my notebook. I feel so bad for Noah. Now I have two reasons to solve this mystery—three, if you count helping my mom get her big break.

Unfortunately I'm no closer to figuring it out.

Chapter 25

The weekend at the farm is so hot, my sisters and I spend most of our time on the dock, swimming, reading, and listening to tunes. Calla forgets all about scavenging for crabs. Bronwyn stays put instead of going to the trouble of meeting up with friends.

By Sunday afternoon, it looks like we've set up camp. We've got towel "beds" with life-jacket pillows, sunscreen, hats, sunglasses, water bottles, and snacks. Lots of snacks. What we don't have is Dad pestering us to help him with a project or Grana's nagging.

Calla imitates Grana: "I can't believe you girls don't fight harder to be here for the summer. I know you're here on weekends, but . . ."

Even though it's only partly funny, it feels good to laugh along with my sisters.

"And Bronwyn," Calla continues, "you really should set your standards higher. That boy, Finn—he isn't going anywhere."

"Well," says Bronwyn, adjusting the bottom of her bathing suit, "Grana was right about that."

"Good riddance," Calla says in her own voice, and that quiets us down again.

I listen to the waves lapping against the dock and the rocking of *Silly Whim*. The sun's warmth on my fingers and toes and the scents of salt, pine, and lotion make me feel the most relaxed I've felt since Gray's accident.

"Yup," Bronwyn says after a few minutes. "Seeing him with Lyndsay was the last straw."

Last straw. Mari has a theory that even if a couple has a million reasons for splitting, there's usually one specific thing that puts the breakup in motion. Like her mother crushing on her Portuguese language teacher. She'd asked me what my parents' one specific thing was but I didn't have a clue, and I was too scared to ask my mom. After all, it's one of those things you really want to know but also don't want to know.

"What was Mom's last straw?" I ask, deciding that today is a want-to-know day.

"Could've been anything," Calla says. "Maybe Dad not listening?"

"I don't think that counts as a last straw," I say. "Too general."

"Besides," says Bronwyn, "he listens. He listens to *us*."

"Maybe," Calla says. "But his listening to *us* reinforced how much he didn't care about *her*."

They fall silent, and I assume the subject is dropped. Then Bronwyn says in a hush, "Grandpa's funeral."

"What about it?" Calla asks, rooting through the snack bag.

"Mom's last straw," says Bronwyn.

I consider this. "You mean because Dad didn't go?" I ask. "He had to make deliveries. Besides, he and Grandpa didn't even like each other."

"Yeah," says Bronwyn, sitting up. "I didn't get it until now, either."

"What?" I ask, propping myself up on my elbows.

"Going to Grandpa's funeral wouldn't have been for Grandpa," Calla realizes.

"Who would it have been f—?"

Oh.

Yeah.

Last straw.

Dinner is a cookout on the back patio. We're having watermelon gazpacho (one of my very favorite foods on this planet) and grilled vegetable quesadillas. You can tell that Dad's really happy to have all three of us here for dinner—he keeps making corny jokes.

"Have you heard from your friend Mari?" Grana

asks me over apple cake. Bronwyn and Calla have already cleared their plates and moved inside, and Dad is washing dishes in the kitchen.

I nod, not wanting to share the fact that I haven't heard from Mari lately—not since she said she'd call me back. "She's having a lot of fun with her cousins," I say.

"You must miss her," says Grana.

"Definitely."

What I don't say is that I want to tell Mari about the conversation I had with Noah, and Bronwyn's revelation about Mom and Dad, but knowing that she's not sharing meaningful stuff with me has been shutting me down.

I ignore Grana's eye roll when I pull out my phone and scroll through my texts with Mari, looking for clues about why things suddenly got so weird between us. I guess I didn't ask her much about Jared; I was so busy filling her in on Gray. I wince a bit when I reread my quote about fine feathers not making fine birds. I was joking—mostly. But maybe she didn't see it that way? And then I went and grouched at her for not telling me about her first kiss right away and asked if Jared checked off enough items on her boyfriend list. Maybe she took all of this as criticism. (Was it?) I think of the quote by Abraham Lincoln: "He has a right to criticize, who has a heart to help."

I have a heart to help! If I criticize Mari or make suggestions like being cautious with someone older or checking her boyfriend list, it's only because I want her to be happy—to be her best self, too. Isn't that the right thing for a friend to do?

We were supposed to be planning our fall wardrobes together this summer, and now I'm beginning to wonder if we're even going to be friends in the fall. Suddenly I recall the look that L&J shared in the supermarket. Maybe Lilliam knows what's wrong—and what I can do to fix it.

> Me: Hey, Lilliam. Has Mari said anything to you about me?
> Lilliam: Like what?
> Me: Have I annoyed her or anything?
> Lilliam: Have you sent her quotes? Haha! JK
> Me: She doesn't like my quotes??
> Lilliam: Not so much

I duck my head so that Grana can't see my expression and ask me what's wrong. With trembling hands, I text:

> Me: Anything else?
> Lilliam: You should talk to her.
> Me: I will. Any advice?
> Lilliam: Don't try so hard to be perfect?

I want to scream, *What?!* Instead, I remember the high road and text back *Thanks!*

The phone feels hot in my hands. I can't believe Mari complained to L&J about me! Why didn't she talk to me directly? And how does my trying to be perfect hurt Mari? I think of my favorite friendship quote: "A friend is someone who understands your past, believes in your future, and accepts you just the way you are."

I accept her the way she is . . . well, sort of. Does encouraging Mari to be her best self translate as criticism, the opposite of acceptance?

I've got to figure out a way to talk to my best friend. Really talk to her. I just hope that nothing I've done so far was her last straw.

> Me: I'm sorry I haven't been a great friend.
>
> Let's talk soon.

I feel disappointed when I don't get an immediate response, but my text is a place to start.

Chapter 26

When I get to the hospital on Monday morning, Mr. Olsen is sitting in the chair next to Gray's bed.

"Oh, Peyton," he says, taking off his glasses. "I guess Kathryn forgot to call you. I decided to stay an extra day."

My heart sinks a little. I was looking forward to telling Gray that I texted with Noah and he seemed like a really cool kid, that I could see why the two of them were friends. I suppose I could say all of this in front of Mr. Olsen, but I don't want to upset him by referring to the accident. Besides, it's something Gray and I can share—something of our own.

"Oh, I brought something!" I say instead. I reach into my backpack and pull out a windup penguin I brought from the farm. "I know Gray has a collection, and I thought it might be fun if it were here for him if—*when* he wakes up."

Mr. Olsen chuckles. "Gray hasn't played with windup toys in years. I'm not sure he has his anymore.

He was—he *is* a rather ambitious boy. Not much for frivolity."

I'm ambitious, too! I want to say. *You should see the quotes on my wall and the lists of goals I keep during the school year.* But then, maybe my standing here holding a windup penguin says otherwise. I slip it into my backpack.

A long silence follows, broken only by the sounds of the monitors.

"Well, tell Mrs. Olsen I said hi," I say, and turn to leave.

"I will," he says, "but she'll probably be back momentarily if you want to stay."

To my surprise, I don't. "That's okay," I say. "I'll be back tomorrow."

But when I reach the waiting area, I have second thoughts. I'm feeling kind of down, and I can't pinpoint the reason. Mrs. Olsen always makes me feel like part of the family. I didn't get that feeling at all from Gray's father. I sit down in one of the chairs for a moment. Maybe it would be good for me to see Mrs. Olsen after all.

I feel someone staring at me and look up. It's the older woman I saw the first time I sat in this waiting area, the one who maybe works at the IGA. Since then, I've bypassed this area and gone directly down the hall to Gray's room. Has this woman been here every day for eleven days? (I'm keeping close track of the number of days Gray has been in a coma.)

I recall the article I read—the one about the woman who kept calling the nurses' station to see how the person she'd hit with her car was doing. What if this woman is doing a similar thing? Maybe she thinks sitting here is a way of praying, of keeping Gray alive.

Something else clicks into place: Noah told me that an older woman was having trouble buying donuts the day Gray was hit. Maybe she was that woman. Maybe she had such a hard time placing her order because just minutes earlier, she had hit Gray!

This moment, too, feels like destiny. I rehearse some words in my head, and then I approach. The chair next to her is free, so I sit on the edge.

"I'm Peyton," I say. "We've been here together before."

"Yes," she says, recognition dawning on her face. "You are the girl who found the camper in the road."

Omigod, she *is* interested in Gray!

"I'm Sonya Turner," she says. "I couldn't help overhearing your conversation with the camp director. That must have been scary for you, coming upon the boy like that."

"It was," I say. For the first time since it happened, I don't feel the urge to retell the story. I'm too jittery. "Are you waiting for news about Gray?" I didn't plan to ask so forthrightly; the question just pushed its way out.

"Gray?" She looks confused. "Oh, the camper. No. I'm here because my wife is here. She had a stroke. I sit in the waiting area when her family visits to give them privacy."

"I'm sorry," I say, and I genuinely mean it. This woman may lose her wife, and here I am, trying to frame her for a potential homicide—just like I did with Mrs. Wagner and Jax. "Has she been here long?"

She takes a tissue from the box on the table next to her. "Since the day the boy arrived. She was reaching for the extra blanket when it happened. It's funny that I remember that. We remember odd things when under stress—do strange things, too. I was sitting here, waiting for Evie to get out of surgery, when I thought, 'I have to buy donuts. Her sister is coming, and she likes Boston cream donuts.'"

Omigod! This *is* the woman Noah saw! Is it possible . . . ?

"I think I've seen you at the IGA," I say, trying to keep my voice calm, casual. "Do you work there?"

"I don't," she says, "but it's possible I've seen you there. You look familiar to me, too. I was thinking that perhaps I saw you at Cecelia Hobbs's annual barbecue last summer. You and your sisters, maybe? My wife and I rent the Parson place."

Omigod! They live down by Mrs. Wagner. She could have been rushing to the hospital that morning, and she was clearly distressed . . .

Suddenly I can hardly breathe. I have to tell Mom.

I make myself stand slowly, trying to act normal. "I hope your wife is better soon."

"Oh," she says, sitting up taller and giving me a small smile, "she's doing much better now. In fact, she's no longer on this floor. I just come up here because it feels familiar—this chair, this view. It all began to feel like mine. Silly, right?"

"Not silly," I say. Not silly for someone who, perhaps even subconsciously, knows that she might have fatally injured a boy.

Chapter 27

"What?" Mom asks as I come racing into the dining room. She's got her laptop open, a smoothie by her side, and papers everywhere.

My fingers itch to tidy them, but I don't. "I think I know who hit Gray."

I don't let her glare, her emphatic sigh, or her slumped shoulders deter me.

"I know you don't want me to be obsessed with solving this case, but you have to admit that I'm probably the perfect one to do it. I'm the one who's at the hospital every day, watching people's behavior, right?"

"And whose behavior have you been watching?"

It's my opening. "Do you know Sonya Turner?" I ask.

"Aren't she and her wife renting the Parson place?"

"Yes! And—" I take a deep breath to calm myself. What I'm about to say is super serious. "And her wife had a stroke. On the morning Gray was hit."

It takes a moment for Mom to register what I'm suggesting. "Peyton, lots of people travel this road. Do you have more?"

"Noah Easton—that's the boy who was in the kayak."

"I know who Noah Easton is. You talked to him?"

I nod, knowing she can't be that mad at me if I solve this mystery. If she's the one who can take this discovery to the police. If she's the one who can write about it first.

"He saw a woman who was distressed while he was at Day's, waiting for Gray to show up."

"I don't recall seeing Ms. Turner at Day's," she says with uncertainty. "How do you know that it was the same—?"

"Ms. Turner told me. She was buying donuts for her sister-in-law. Boston cream," I add, knowing that this detail adds legitimacy to my story.

Mom stops acting like I'm the criminal here.

"Did Ms. Turner tell you what time she drove her wife to the hospital? Or if she even drove? Maybe her wife went by ambulance."

I shake my head. "I was afraid that if I asked more questions, she'd get upset. But she went to the hospital. She had to get there somehow, right?"

Mom grabs her notebook and pen and then calls Cecelia Hobbs. She chats with Cecelia casually, letting the conversation turn naturally to Sonya's wife, Evie, and details about her stroke. Every now and then, she jots something down in her notebook. I want to see what she's writing, but I don't dare distract her.

When she gets off the call, I learn that Evie went to the hospital by ambulance at around four a.m. and Sonya immediately followed in her car. That's long before Gray was hit.

I expect Mom to head to the laundry room to put in a load or to tell me to pack up my things to go to the farm right now. But she surprises me by pulling me in for a hug. "You and I are a lot alike," she says. I realize that even though I've been deep-down fearing our sameness, I also feel a little proud in this moment.

"But," she says, "I need you to promise me that you'll stop doing your own investigating."

"But you said yourself that the police have moved on to other cases! And I don't see you working on it, either. It can't go unsolved."

"I have to write other things, Peyton, or I can't pay the bills. It doesn't mean I've given up. You saw how quickly I called Cecelia just now. But I am your mother, and investigating a hit-and-skip case is not a healthy activity for a twelve"—she pauses and smiles—"almost-thirteen-year-old. I want you to stop."

I don't know what to say. I want to promise my

mother, but I also promised Gray. How can I keep both?

"I'll do my best," I say.

"That's all I ask."

The next morning, I'm sitting next to Gray and notice that they've changed his hospital gown again. He's wearing a sky-blue one today, and it makes my heart pang. I'm not sure why—maybe it's just a simple sign that people aren't giving up. They remember that there is a boy trapped in this body.

"Hey, Gray," I say. "I'm here." For some reason, I picture us in a movie. I'm sitting at Gray's bedside, talking softly. Suddenly he opens his eyes and looks right up at me. Looks up and smiles. It's a smile of recognition. A smile that says, *Oh, it's you. You're the one.*

And I smile back.

But apart from the gown, Gray doesn't look much different from how he did the day before or the day before that.

I pull out my phone and look at the calendar. I remember Mrs. Olsen saying that people have a far greater chance of coming out of a coma within the first couple of weeks. After that, their chances drop. It's Tuesday, July ninth. It will be two weeks on Thursday.

My worried thoughts are interrupted by one of the nurses walking in the door. She's younger than most of the nurses I see on this floor and has her hair up in a messy bun.

"Hi, Peyton," she says, and I'm surprised she knows my name. "It's good of you to keep Gray company." She checks his pulse, makes sure all of his tubes and pouches are working as they should.

"Have you ever seen Gray move?" I ask, looking for reassurance.

"Once," she says. "But it was reactive. Nonvoluntary." I can tell she's used to managing people's hopes.

"Did it scare you?"

She looks at me as if perhaps I've been asked to do something too difficult for someone my age, so I quickly clarify, "I mean, did you startle?"

She smiles. "Yup," she says. "I jumped a mile. It's just unexpected."

I nod, knowingly.

She starts for the door, but pauses. "Are you hungry?" she asks. "We've got pudding and Fudgsicles in the fridge behind the nurses' station."

A Fudgsicle would be yummy, but I'm afraid I'd drip on Gray's photo book, which I haven't even opened yet. Plus it would be hard to tell stories or describe things with food in my mouth. "No, thanks," I say. "I'm good."

"Okay," she says, smiling again. Then, before leaving, she stops at a control panel near the door. "Do you want some tunes in here?"

I hadn't realized they could play music in the room. It's never been on when I've stopped by, and I wonder if Mr. and Mrs. Olsen prefer it that way.

Without waiting for an answer, she turns a dial, and suddenly music starts playing from a speaker in the wall. I wonder if she picked the playlist this morning, because this song is definitely better than the one I heard in the waiting area on the day Gray was hit.

"My name is Carrie, if you need anything," she says, and then she's gone.

"It's just you and me again, Gray."

I peek in the back of his photo book to see if there are any new cards, and sure enough, there's one in a blue envelope.

It's from a bunch of kids. It's filled with separate messages, all hoping Gray gets better soon. I read them aloud, glancing up at Gray to see if he's reacting. There are lots of messages from girls, lots and lots of hearts. There's one that reads, "I miss my best friend." I stumble over the signature: *Jordan*. Guy or girl? I can't be sure.

"You have a card from Jordan, who misses you," I tell Gray. "I miss my best friend, too. She's away for the summer. Mari can be funny. Sometimes she says outrageous things, but then she'll come out with something really truthful, really wise. And she's messy, but she can put together the most creative outfits." I sigh. "But I think I might have blown it with her. I think maybe I'm too . . . I don't know, too careful? Too neat? Maybe just too obnoxious."

I swear, in that moment, emotion passes over his face. Like he is telling me not to feel that way, that I'm not a pain, that it's good to care about things.

I take a deep breath and relax.

I put the card back in the photo book and am searching for a new picture—something I haven't seen before—when "Try, Try, Try" comes over the speaker. Mari's and my song! It's like a sign from the universe! I sing along softly. *"You gotta try, try, try to fly, fly, fly. Fly—"*

There's a picture of Gray in a Cub Scout uniform. He's got a pinewood derby car in one hand and a little trophy in the other. I slide my glasses down my nose and hold the book closer to see if I can tell what place he got. "Nice work on the Cub Scouts derby!" I tell him. "First place—cool!"

I flip through more pages. *"You gotta try, try, try to fly, fly, fly. Fly—let your dreams soar!"*

Bang!

Omigod! Gray's fingers are fluttering!

And he's smiling! This doesn't look like random

motion. It looks like he's reacting to the song.

I fumble for the call button while I sing louder. His shoulders begin to rock gently.

I press the call button, then grab his hand. *"You gotta try, try, try to fly, fly, fly,"* I sing, waving his hand in mine. *"You gotta try, try, try . . ."*

Gray's shoulders still. I'm about to let go when . . .

He squeezes my hand!

"Omigod! Omigod!"

He's holding my fingers so tightly, there can be no doubt it's a deliberate action!

"Nurse Carrie!" I call. "Mr. and Mrs. Olsen! Come quick!"

Nurse Carrie comes rushing in. "He squeezed my hand!" I cry. "And he was dancing—sort of dancing, I mean. Moving to the music!"

She examines Gray, whose eyes are still closed. As she talks to him, though, his face contorts. She looks at me, and her smile is nearly blinding. She checks something on the monitor and uses her pager to call a doctor.

The song coming from the speaker changes, and Gray lets go of my hand.

"He responded to your voice," Carrie says to me, replacing her pager and checking to make sure nothing has come loose on Gray. "Keep talking to him."

"I think it was the song," I say. As much as I want

it to be my voice that woke him up, he didn't react at all until "Try, Try, Try" came on. *"Fly—let your dreams soar,"* I sing, testing my theory.

He wiggles again!

The doctor rushes in while I'm singing to Gray. So do his parents. There's a lot of commotion. I move away from the bed. Mr. and Mrs. Olsen take turns talking to Gray.

And then it happens.

He opens his eyes.

Omigod!

"Gray!" Mrs. Olsen gushes.

I crane to get a better look at him. Is there recognition in his eyes, or are they clouded with confusion? I want to know that he's not only going to live, but that he's going to be okay.

And I want to be a part of this moment—this moment when the boy I care about most reenters this world.

But Carrie takes me by the shoulders and gently guides me out of the room.

"Let's get that Fudgsicle now," she says. "That was a brave and wonderful thing you did there, and later, everyone will come to understand that you helped bring that boy back."

I reach out and hug her.

Chapter 28

I watched a movie once in which a patient woke up from a coma. In the movie, the kid didn't know where he was or remember what had happened, but otherwise he was pretty normal. He recognized people, could talk, and was out of bed within hours.

In real life, most people come out of comas gradually. (That is, if they come out at all.) I know this because Mom immediately went into research mode when I came home with the news that Gray was awake—or was at least in the process of waking. She wanted to write a short article about his recovery but didn't want to jump the gun. Together we read about how for many coma patients, the road to recovery can take weeks or months, and that it may be a back-and-forth process. One day the patient may seem to understand what's going on, and the next he may seem lost.

I wake up the next day eager to get back to the hospital—to see Gray, to talk to him properly for the first time.

Mom suggests I stay home for a day or two to give the family time. "He probably can't have visitors yet," she says.

"That's okay," I lie. "It's my job, and Mrs. Olsen didn't tell me not to come at my usual time. I might not be needed, but it would be irresponsible not to show up."

Mom gives me her *I'm not buying this* look.

"I just want to be there," I plead. "My insides feel like they're going to explode! I've been sitting next to him and talking to him every day. And now that he's awake, I need to be there. To hear how he's doing. To know if he's okay."

Though she still looks pretty conflicted, she gives in. "No more than one hour. Even if Gray can have visitors. You are not to hang around there today."

"Agreed!"

"How are you doing, little one?" Ahmed says as I approach the desk.

"Not so little," I say. "How is Gray doing?"

"I am only allowed to tell you two things," Ahmed says. "Hospital rules."

"Any two things?" I ask. What a ridiculous rule!

Ahmed laughs. "No, for patient privacy, I may only tell you how he is doing—in one word—and what floor he's on."

"Oh," I say, but then quickly decide that's good information.

Ahmed goes to his screen. "He's in *fair* condition."

"That's good, right?"

Ahmed looks up from his screen and smiles. "Yes. Fair is good."

"And what floor is he on?" I ask.

"Pediatric," he says. "It's on the second floor," he adds when he sees me hesitating.

I nod. I know that already. It's the same floor as my doctor's office and the cafeteria and gift shop. I'm hesitating because I realize that I might, in just one short flight, actually talk to Gray for the first time.

Maybe Mom's right. Maybe I should wait. Wait until he's had a little more time to recover. I don't really know what *fair* means. Does it mean that he'll be sitting up and speaking, carrying on conversations? Or does it mean awake but not much else?

"Thanks, Ahmed," I say, knowing that he's told me all he can. I turn to head home.

But then I stop.

At home I'll spend all my time wanting to be here.

I reverse direction again and head to the stairwell.

"Good luck," Ahmed says, seeming to understand the courage this requires.

When I reach the top of the stairs, I turn left, away

from my doctor's office and into another wing. I walk beside a woman and two kids. She's carrying a teddy bear. Each of the kids has a wrapped package that's undoubtedly a book. I kick myself for forgetting a gift. Is the windup penguin still in my backpack?

It doesn't matter. I wouldn't dare give it to Gray now, after his father shared his thoughts.

Why didn't I think of this? Or at least bring more money so I could get something at the gift shop?

No sooner have I entered the unfamiliar waiting room than I realize that these are not the nurses who know me—the ones who have greeted me every day, who have been happy to answer my questions.

"May I help you?" the nurse at the desk asks.

My heart slams against my chest. "I'm here to see Gray. Gray Olsen."

"I'm sorry," she says, "but Gray isn't receiving visitors today."

I glance around to see if Mrs. Olsen is nearby, by chance. No sighting.

"I'm the girl who called the ambulance," I tell her. "I was with him when he woke up. His mom hired me to tell him stories." I say all this hoping that she's heard of me, that she'll realize I've been allowed into his room all along. "Mrs. Olsen may be expecting me," I add.

She seems unmoved, but she takes a moment to

glance at her monitor. "Sorry, sweetie. Parents are the only visitors allowed today." Then she leans closer to me and says with a wrinkled nose, "A lot of testing is going on," and I instantly like her, though I wonder if she's breaking the privacy rules.

As soon as I have that thought, I imagine Mari rolling her eyes at my insistence on perfect rule-following.

Right's right, I think, but then I soften, recalling my recent trespassing. *Those who live in glass houses should not throw stones.*

I could text Mrs. Olsen, but if Gray's undergoing a lot of tests today, I don't want to be in the way. Besides, waiting a day or two will give me a chance to prepare. I decide to go to the gift shop and choose something to purchase the next time I come.

As I'm heading into the gift shop, I nearly bump into a woman coming out.

It's Ms. Turner! Shame grabs hold of me as I remember that I thought she was capable of leaving a boy to die.

"Peyton!" she says. "I heard that the boy is awake!"

"I was with him when it happened," I tell her. "He reacted to the music that was playing on the speaker."

Ms. Turner purses her lips in a knowing way and nods steadily. "Music can be so powerful. And you were with him. What an eventful summer you are having!"

"Hey, I know her!" a man's voice booms from down the hall.

We turn to see Jax and his grandfather approaching.

"Why, hello!" Ms. Turner says, and then to me, "Do you know Mr. McCallister and his grandson, Jackson? We met in the cafeteria one day."

Again, I am stricken with shame. Shame and something else. Embarrassment? I think of the way I talked to Jax in the cafeteria, the way I assumed he thought life was a joke, and all along he was caring for his sick grandfather.

Another couple tries to pass our group in the hall. Mr. McCallister takes Ms. Turner's arm and guides her toward the gift shop's far window, leaving Jax and me standing alone by the door.

I feel like I should apologize, but then I'd have to admit to the terrible things I was thinking.

Mr. McCallister is talking loudly about something that happened when he was a kid. Jax looks embarrassed.

"Cecelia Hobbs told me you've been helping out your grandfather," I say.

Jax's face reddens. "He forgets things. Gets confused. He's probably telling Ms. Turner this story because he can't remember *how* they know each other and he's afraid she'll figure it out."

"Did his memory loss happen all at once?" I ask.

He shakes his head. "It's a slow progression. You would think that would be easier, but I hate it. I'm watching one of my best friends disappear, bit by bit."

I notice how tired he looks, especially around the eyes. "I saw you at the fair," I say. "Those terrible pitches were a clever way to distract him."

Jax rolls his eyes, a little bit embarrassed, a little bit proud of his quick thinking.

"Hey, wait," he says, reaching into his pocket. "I think I have something of yours."

As soon as I see the tip of the familiar white stationery, I know exactly what it is. Now it's my turn to be thoroughly embarrassed. I think of number one—*must be cute*—and feel so silly, so exposed.

"I picked this up near your feet," he says, handing it to me. "Normally I would have given it back to you right away, but I was so embarrassed. I didn't want to stay near that line for another moment." Then he quickly adds, "I didn't read it, though."

Yeah, right. Who would pick up a piece of folded paper and not read it? I certainly would have. I slip the list into my back pocket, making sure it's secure, then squint at him, waiting to see if I can get him to confess under pressure. But then Mr. McCallister's voice rises. "It's not easy taking care of a fourteen-year-old boy!"

Jax throws his head back as if to say, *Here it comes.*

"The boy watches too much TV. Eats constantly. But that's not the worst of it. He has no respect for my property—isn't that right, Jackson? Why, just the other night . . ."

Jax looks stricken, and for a moment, I think he's going to bolt.

"There you are!" says Cecelia Hobbs, coming down the hall. "I knew something—or someone—must have waylaid the two of you." She turns to Ms. Turner. "Sonya, hi. How's Evie?"

"I'll meet you downstairs," Jax says to Cecelia, and he hurries away.

I can't believe what I've just seen and heard. Jax was definitely frightened by what his grandfather was saying. I can't help thinking that "property" might mean a car. Maybe my earlier suspicions were correct after all.

I race down the stairs and rush through the main lobby.

"Hey, little one—"

"Not so little!" I shout to Ahmed as I race past him. I can see Jax under the awning, waiting for Cecelia.

I slow down, not wanting to scare him off.

But as soon as the automatic doors open and he sees me, he takes off across the parking lot.

"Wait!" I yell. I can't let him get away—not this time. Not when I might finally, *finally* know the truth about what happened to Gray.

I run after him.

Chapter 29

"What happened to you?" Mom asks when I come limping through the front door.

I touch the side of my face and wince. "I tripped in the parking lot."

I'm so tempted to tell her about Jax, but I don't. Twice now, I have shared my suspicions. Twice I have been wrong. That, and I promised her I'd stop trying to solve this mystery.

This time I need hard evidence, I decide as she helps me clean the cuts on my face and both my knees. I need to find the car, take pictures. After looking up the address, I could bike out to Old Post Road to find the McCallister house.

I must admit, though, that I feel bad for Jax, having to take care of his grandfather. I don't know what I'd do if I were stuck in a house with a man like that all summer. Heck, maybe I'd even borrow my grandfather's car to get away for a while. (Not likely!)

One thing's for sure, though—if I accidentally hit

somebody, I would *never* drive away. No matter how badly I might want to.

Mrs. Olsen texts the next morning and says that Gray would love to meet me on the following day. I almost say no. I want to see him so badly, but I have this ridiculous red-and-purple scrape on my face, and that's *not* how I want to look when he sees me for the first time.

It isn't until Calla points out that I've been staring at him for a week with gashes, cuts, and tubes that I realize I'm not exactly being fair.

"You've come to the right person," Bronwyn says when I ask her to help me cover the mess with makeup on Friday morning. You can still see it after she spends oodles of time rubbing and patting, but it's definitely better.

I put on a green sundress that used to belong to Calla. It has wide straps and big pockets, and I almost feel pretty.

Mom decides to go with me. She wants to talk with the Olsens.

I still don't have a gift for Gray, but I have his sunglasses to return. I decide that they're even better than a random present.

We enter the lobby, and the familiar smell of the

hospital—a combination of cleaning fluid and something flowery—makes me feel like I've arrived at my third home.

Ahmed gives us Gray's new room number, and Mom and I decide to take the stairs instead of the elevator. Was it just two weeks ago that I hobbled through this hospital with an injured ankle?

I'm not at all prepared for what I see when we go through the waiting area and down the hall. There's a crowd of kids my age parked outside the room I'm guessing belongs to Gray. Everywhere I look, there are stuffed animals and balloons. Kids are holding up get-well signs and snapping selfies. They must be his friends from Connecticut. I wonder how they got here. Who drove them? I could tell from his photo book and all the cards and letters he got that he's popular, but this is beyond amazing.

I feel funny walking through this crowd to his room. Should I ask if I need to wait my turn?

Mom doesn't have the same reservations. She works her way through the crowd and gives a little knock on Gray's partially open door, and we head in. Unlike Gray's ICU room, this one is filled with flowers and get-well cards and baseball paraphernalia. (Baseball! How could I not have known that he's a big fan? Gray's triple play was one of the first stories Mrs. Olsen shared. I'm both envious of his friends for knowing and mad at myself for not realizing it sooner.)

Gray's small room is equally crowded with people. In addition to Gray's parents, there are other family members gathered inside. I recognize them from Gray's photo book, and I wonder if they've come all the way from Norway.

I steal a glance at Gray. He hasn't noticed me yet. He's sitting up and looking very alert for someone who's just come out of a coma. His bandages have been removed, and his hair's washed and combed. He's even dressed in a clean button-down shirt! He's smiling at a group of kids of different ages who seem to be recounting something that happened in the cafeteria.

It's so odd to see him awake. I've been staring at this face for weeks and yet am only now seeing the way he scrunches his forehead when he listens and tilts his head back when he laughs.

Mr. Olsen is the first to notice we've arrived. "Here she is!" he shouts, and everyone looks our way. A man and a woman carrying a TV camera are standing beside him. I was so intent on seeing Gray, I didn't notice them before.

Mrs. Olsen introduces the man to my mother. "This is—"

"Hal Lindstrom," my mother says before Mrs. Olsen can finish.

Of course my mother knows Mr. Lindstrom. He's the anchor at Channel 5 News. He and Mom often cover the same stories.

"Tally!" he says. "It's good to see you." Then, before Mom has a chance to answer, he lowers his voice and says, "If I'm not mistaken, your daughter not only found this young man but helped bring him out of a coma."

It's only at this moment that I realize my mother has been sitting on a great human-interest story. A story that is significant not only to Channel 5 but would likely make the front page of any of the big papers. But she hasn't acted on it.

I glance around the room. A girl about my age is staring at me, but Gray seems to be looking at some baseball cards. Does he even know I'm here?

His face looks like it has more color. His little dog—the one Mrs. Olsen placed next to him in bed—is hanging from a hose that's not in use. And by hanging, I mean by its neck. No doubt one of his friends did this. I hope it doesn't upset him too much to see his buddy treated this way.

"I hope you don't mind, Tally," Mrs. Olsen says. "We're still trying to find the driver of the vehicle. We thought that running a news story about the role that Peyton played in saving Gray's life—and about them meeting for the first time—would keep the story fresh in the public's mind and keep the case hot."

She then turns to me. "Thoughts, Peyton? We've already spoken to Gray, and he's agreed to being on camera."

I look up at my mother, who is wearing a neutral expression—a blank look that Bronwyn claims she perfected while living with Grana. Why didn't Mrs. Olsen ask my mother to cover the story first? I'm feeling a bit prickly on her behalf.

"How do you feel about that?" Mom asks me.

I look over at Gray, who at the same moment looks up at me, and . . . we lock eyes.

My heart thrums faster, and I want to look away, but I don't. I wait.

I wait until this weird shyness I'm feeling is overtaken by joy. Gray's awake, and he's looking right at me.

I smile.

Gray doesn't return the smile. Which is perfectly understandable. He hasn't truly met me yet—not while he's awake. But his eyes stay locked on mine. They seem to be pleading. This news story matters to him. Finding the driver matters to him. Maybe this is one way I *can* keep my promise to both my mother and Gray.

"Okay," I say.

Gray gives a little nod and looks back down at his cards.

Mrs. Olsen smiles warmly. The camerawoman gets into position, and Mr. Lindstrom tells me where to stand next to Gray's bed. "When I give you the signal," he says, "go ahead and introduce yourself to Gray."

This is not how I expected this afternoon would go. But maybe, I think, we'll tell this story to our grandkids one day and show them the footage.

Mr. Lindstrom raises and drops his finger.

"Hi, Gray," I say, and my voice wobbles. How many times have I said that now? I hope that deep down in his heart, he remembers. "I'm Peyton." I think of holding out my hand, but it feels too weird.

Finally he gives me a quirky smile. "So, you're the one who found me in the road."

I nod. The shyness has returned, but I push forward. "I was riding my bike."

The reporter gives me a nod that says, *Go on.*

"At first, I thought you were a pile of clothes. But I circled back, and there you were. I was so shocked!"

"Thanks," he says. "Thanks for turning around."

The room erupts in little sounds of approval. I swear I can feel the smiles.

"Peyton," he says, and the whole room quiets again. The camerawoman takes a step closer. "I hope my face didn't look as bad as yours does right now."

Chapter 30

That evening, while my sisters and I are at the farm eating crab dip and chips and waiting for the six o'clock news with my story to come on, I ask Dad if he'll drive me to the hospital tomorrow.

I cringe when I think of what Gray said about my face, but I'm sure he was feeling just as nervous as I was and trying to be funny. Mrs. Olsen came forward and put her arm around me and said, "He's not fully himself yet." Then she told me that most of the kids from Connecticut would be heading up to Acadia tomorrow—their families had decided to make a weekend of visiting Maine—and that I'd have a chance to talk with Gray "with less commotion." I couldn't tell if she said it because she thought Gray and I had something special or because she'd grown fond of me, but either way, it made me happy.

"You've just arrived, and already you're making plans to go back into town?" Grana asks.

"Mrs. Olsen invited me. I could hardly talk to

Gray today with the news cameras and all the other visitors. I'd like to try again tomorrow."

"Of course," says Dad. "What time do you want to go?"

Grana ignores him. "But we've got the farmers market, and then I thought you girls and I would go strawberry picking. We haven't done that yet, and they won't last much longer."

"Can't," Calla says. "Aunt Beth is taking me to the blues festival."

"Play rehearsal," says Bronwyn. I'm pretty sure my grandmother already knows their plans.

Grana looks at me. "Looks like it's just you and me, my sweet camellia," Grana says, like it's all decided. "We can make jam when we get back."

"Mom," Dad says with an edge in his voice, "you just heard me tell Peyton that I'll take her to the hospital."

"Well, you didn't think it through. Peyton loves strawberries." She smiles at me, as if to say, *Don't you, Peyton*? "Besides, I thought we agreed that you were going to let this boy—"

"It's okay," I say, not wanting to get into a discussion about whether or not it's healthy for me to want to spend time with Gray.

"It's not okay," says Dad, banging his glass on the coffee table. "You heard Peyton express her desire.

She would like to visit this boy at the hospital again."

"I'm just trying to be helpful, David. The season goes by so quickly—"

"You're not being helpful, Mom. You're bullying. Let Peyton have a voice."

"Bullying! Is that what you think I'm doing, Peyton?"

Dad takes a deep breath. "You're constantly forcing her to choose sides, Mom. To choose you. Stop it."

Grana's lips compress. She picks up her glass and goes into her bedroom.

Dad goes into the kitchen to refill his glass.

Bronwyn, Calla, and I are a bit stunned.

I expect to feel sad that Grana is upset. But I don't. I try to think of a quote that will soothe my guilt—my guilt about not feeling sadder for my grandmother. My grandmother, whom I love. I can't think of one. So I make one up: "Sometimes, things have to be said."

A teaser about a girl who quite possibly saved a boy's life comes on TV, and Calla calls for my grandmother and Dad to return quickly.

Dad comes rushing in. Grana does not, but we can hear the news program playing on her laptop in the other room.

"Look! There you are!" squeals Bronwyn.

The news segment opens with a view of Winding Lane and Hal Lindstrom's voice-over, telling about the accident and how I found Gray. After that, they show our meeting—we don't look nearly as nervous as I felt—and then my interview, where I talk about how I told Gray stories about his life using the photo book. I also tell about singing "Try, Try, Try," the song that woke Gray up.

Next they show an interview they did with Gray. (Did they do it before I arrived?) He said that he and his best friend back in Connecticut used to clown around to "Try, Try, Try." They played the song in the hospital room, and Gray said, "This is for you, Jordan," and made these corny arm motions. (I kind of wish they'd left this part out.) Last, Hal Lindstrom talks about the power of music and how it has awakened many people—some quite famous—from comas.

The whole segment is available for streaming immediately after. I send Mari a link along with a text that says that I know I've talked a lot about myself this summer, and this video is about me, too, but I can't imagine not sharing it with my best friend. I haven't heard back by the time I slip into bed, but I've stopped being surprised.

Which makes me feel incredibly sad.

Maybe she really is through with me.

Or maybe it's even worse. Maybe she's been wanting a break from me for some time. Maybe she chose Gloucester for that very reason.

Chapter 31

"Walk down to the farmers market," Dad says as he drops me off, "when you're done with your visit."

I go directly to Gray's room—Ahmed is not at the desk this morning—and am totally surprised to see L&J. They're standing by his bedside and laughing. No Mrs. Olsen in sight.

"Hi, Peyton!" Lilliam says as I approach the bed. "We saw you on TV. It was such a nice thing you did, visiting Gray. We thought we should, too."

"We brought chocolates," says Jamie.

"And a Mussel Cove baseball cap," says Lilliam. Both of these gifts rest on top of Gray's covers.

"I brought something, too, Gray," I say as if we're old friends—which we are, kind of. I mean, I practically know as much about his life as I do about Mari's. I reach into my backpack and pull out the sunglasses. I hold them in the air for a moment, giving him a moment to recognize them, and then pass them to him. They're fairly beaten up, but a pretty good memento of his recent brush with death. They've got to beat a Mussel Cove cap, anyway.

As I hand them to him, I feel a brief pang of loss. Those glasses are tangible proof of all I went through. They are a part of Gray that for a short while belonged to me.

Gray glances at the glasses and then gives L&J a conspiratorial look. Like, *This girl is so weird.*

"You brought him busted-up sunglasses?" asks Jamie.

"Not any busted-up sunglasses. *His* sunglasses."

Gray sits up a little taller in his bed and snickers. "Definitely not mine."

"Yes, they are," I say, coming closer. Maybe Gray's memory isn't completely restored. "I found them just a few feet from where I found you. They were even more bent—I tried to straighten them."

"Oh," says Lilliam, like she gets it now.

Gray makes a smirky face at them, but then there's a moment of recognition. "Wait a minute. These are Connor's—he was a kid in my bunk. I'd been admiring them. I grabbed them as I was running out the door." He laughs. "Guess he won't be getting them back now."

I think of number seven on my boyfriend list: *Must not be sneaky.* But I quickly push the thought away.

He may have been borrowing them, I tell myself. *You don't know.*

"Hey, watch this," Gray says as he tosses the glasses into the air. We watch them swoosh into the wastebasket.

"Great shot!" Jamie says.

He grins. "I know, right?"

"Hey," he says, "would one of you get me one of those blueberry muffins from the cafeteria? The food here sucks."

"We'll get it!" Lilliam says before I can answer.

"Are you sure?" I ask. I feel like I should be the one to do things for Gray.

"We're sure," says Jamie.

The two of them take no time getting out of the room. Maybe they think we'd like to be alone. The thought makes me jittery.

"How are you feeling?" I ask.

He knocks his head back. "I'm so sick of people asking me that."

Ouch. I get that he's tired of being asked that question, but I'm surprised that he finds it equally annoying coming from me.

I breathe in slowly to settle my jitters. "I'm sorry," I say, and mean it. "It's weird—I feel like I know so much about you from your photo book and all, but

I'm realizing now that you probably don't have any memory of—"

Gray reaches for the remote and turns on the TV. "Do you like baseball?" he asks. He flips through the channels until he finds a game. "This actually aired last night, but you should see the play the right fielder made."

I adjust a chair so it faces the TV. Baseball's not my thing, but it's kind of nice that he wants to share it with me. And it makes me realize that my boyfriend list might be a little selfish. I mean, it shouldn't be all about me, right? Maybe his girlfriend list would have "loves baseball" at the top.

I watch and listen. "What's a changeup pitch?" I ask.

"It looks like a fastball, but it isn't."

Huh. "I've never understood what a fastball is," I say. "I mean, don't pitchers want all of their pitches to have speed? Isn't that the point?"

"Just watch," he says.

All of the excitement inside me has trickled out. But I try to hang in there. Where are L&J with that muffin?

"Throw it to second!" he yells. "Second!"

While Gray has an imaginary conversation with the ballplayers—not unlike the imaginary conversations I had with him while he was in a coma—my mind wanders back to my boyfriend list (which is safely tucked in a drawer at home). I think of number eight: *Like to hold hands.* We sort of held hands when he was gaining consciousness. I think of waving his hand in the air and giggle.

He glances over at me, but immediately goes back to watching the game.

To be fair, Gray hasn't had time to accomplish many of the items on my list. He can't very well give me surprises or pose for funny pictures. (Well, he could, but I don't think we're ready for that.) But maybe those aren't the most essential things, either.

I think of number six: *Be a good listener and take me seriously.* That's an important one. I'm pretty certain that if I tell him I think I've solved the mystery of the hit-and-run driver, he'll listen. But that's not a very fair test. Besides, I still want to give the info to my mom first, especially knowing she didn't get yesterday's story. So I try to start another conversation.

"I wish I were better at sports," I say.

Gray holds out the remote and turns the TV off. He looks at me, and I mentally check off number six. It feels good. It feels like he's going to ask me to say more.

"I'm tired," he says. "Would you mind going so I can sleep?"

I become very still. "Of course not," I say, getting

up and angling the chair the way I found it. It's a reasonable request, I tell myself, but it doesn't stop embarrassment (or is it anger?) from rising inside me.

An anger that I immediately extinguish. Of course he's tired. He's probably far from himself. The poor guy was in a near-fatal accident. He's been in a coma for almost two weeks. I feel terrible. "Feel better," I say.

"Yeah," he says. "Will do."

As I'm leaving the hospital, I see Ms. Turner in the parking lot. She's walking hand in hand with another woman. This must be her wife. Evie, I recall. I feel better already.

As I walk to the farmers market, I recall our visit (and wonder if he ever did get that blueberry muffin). I decide to show up with one on Monday, along with the news that the hit-and-run driver has been found—and that I was the one who figured it out.

He'll see the real me then. The one he's destined to love.

Chapter 32

Grana is sitting at the kitchen table reading the *Bangor Daily News*. There's a bouquet of daisies in front of her.

"I know a lot of flowers are flashier," I say, hoping she's over her anger. "More exotic. But I still love daisies best."

"Good to hear," she says coolly, "because the perennial gardens need us. Get ready for deadheading, watering, and mulching." Apparently there will be no strawberry picking today.

Just then Aunt Beth comes in from her morning run. She's breathing hard and glistening with sweat, but her face is shining.

"Nine miles this morning!" she says. Then she looks at me. "If you ever decide to take up running, Peyton, I have an extra pair of shoes your size."

Is she serious? Or is she teasing me about my big feet again? Either way, my answer's the same. "Thanks, but I prefer biking."

"You never kno-ow," she singsongs as she moves in circles to cool down.

Grana looks up. "I hope you drank plenty of water before you left."

"No worries," Aunt Beth says. "I won't wither in the fields."

Aunt Beth goes to stretch and shower, and Grana says, "I'll get you sunscreen, a water bottle, and a hat" as she leaves the room.

"Where's Dad?" I call after her.

"Out delivering!" she calls back.

Before long, I'm knee-deep in pink and purple lupines. The cold, wet spring has caused them to bloom later than usual. I'm trying to figure out a way to search for the McCallister car. I wish I'd thought to bring my bike this weekend. The roads on this side of town are super hilly, so I typically don't want it. But it's almost three miles from the farm to Jax's house, and walking will take forever.

I can't see Grana or Aunt Beth—we've divided up the patch—but I know they're within earshot. I call out, "Aunt Beth, I think I'm going to try running after all!"

"Cool!" she says. "You'll love it! You won't believe how strong you'll feel."

We work for several hours. From time to time, one of us starts singing a song we all know, and the others join in—even Grana. Seems like she's moved past her hurt.

After a lunch of tuna fish sandwiches and lemonade, Grana announces that she's going to take a nap. Aunt Beth is meeting a friend in town, but I stop her in the hall before she leaves and ask if she can put her hands on those old shoes.

"It's not an ideal time of day to run," she says. "It will be so much hotter now than it is in the early morning or evening."

I don't have a quick response. If I wait, I'm afraid there won't be another chance—or that Grana will try to dissuade me.

"On the other hand," Aunt Beth says, "if you get in the habit of waiting for the perfect conditions, you'll never become a runner. I'll get the shoes."

"I won't go too far," I tell her. "And I'll hydrate."

"Cool," she says. "Let me find them."

I waste no time. I throw on a lighter T-shirt, pop on the running shoes (which feel a little awkward, since they're well worn), and drink a full eight ounces of water. I grab the same baseball cap I wore gardening, write a quick note—*Going for a run*—and try hard not to let the door slam on the way out.

Then, as if I believe my lie, I start jogging. I'm not sure how far I'll be able to go in this midday heat, but if Grana looks out the window—*please do not look out the window, Grana!*—she'll be reminded of what I said earlier and know where I'm going. I take off at quite a good clip.

I'm barely beyond the end of our long—and it has never felt so long—driveway before I'm gasping for my life.

There isn't much of a shoulder on this road. I run past trees, low stone walls that used to contain cows back when this land was mostly pasture, and discreet dirt driveways that lead to fine houses along the shore.

I don't get far before I have to slow down and walk. I have got to build up my lung capacity! But then the horseflies hovering around my head annoy me to no end!

So I make up a game. Walk past three telephone poles. Run past three poles. Walk past three poles. Run past three poles.

I'm dripping with sweat. After each running section, I can't tell if it's cicadas I hear or ringing in my ears.

I wish I'd brought my water bottle.

When I get to the intersection that leads to town, I turn right onto Old Post Road and head up a hill. There's no way I'm running this, so I don't bother to count poles.

I trudge, swatting at horseflies along the way. At

the top of the hill, a house sits on each side of the road. One is a split-level with chickens roaming free in the yard, and the other is a little house with a porch on the front. An old man I don't recognize is sitting in an easy chair on that front porch. I start to wave out of habit but stop myself. Just because I don't know who he is doesn't mean *he* doesn't know *me*. What if he recognizes me as Tally Walsh and David Campbell's kid, or worse, Grana's grandkid, and tells them he saw me jogging by?

I'm probably being paranoid, but still, I press on without my usual greeting.

It's not easy to determine house numbers on a rural road. Some mailboxes have them, some don't. Some houses have the number on the front, but most don't. The numbers jump from twenty-seven to thirty-nine to fifty-eight to sixty-three. I'm definitely getting closer. I pull out my phone and use the GPS to confirm.

My stomach is a rolling sea. I hope that Jax's grandfather's house doesn't have a garage. The thought of peeking in someone's window and getting caught again makes me queasy.

I nearly crash into a mailbox that juts out farther than normal—one that's on a swinging bar intended to outwit snowplows. It's number ninety-three!

The house is another split-level with a large picture

window. It sits at the top of a steep driveway with cracked pavement. There's a small patch of lawn in front that's been recently mowed, but the sides of the house are engulfed in tall grasses and weeds. I'm guessing there was a time when the yard was better kept.

My heart jogs up to my throat. There's no car in the driveway, but there is an attached garage.

I've come all this way. I've got to check it out. But how do I look inside without being caught again? There's no way my parents would forgive me for doing this a second time.

Still. What if the damaged car is in that garage? What if justice is finally served?

Experience tells me there is probably a window on the side of the garage that's not attached to the house. I decide to walk past the house altogether and bushwhack up the slope until I can come out of the trees without being seen.

There are pricker bushes alongside the road similar to the *Rosa rugosa* in our backyard. I try to hold the vines out of the way as I walk through them, but they scratch my legs just the same.

Then, wouldn't you know it, as soon as I've made it through the bushes, my feet land in a marshy area. The water seeps into Aunt Beth's old running shoes. I slosh through, hit solid ground, and start pushing my way uphill through the trees. The forest isn't too dense, and I can see the house off to my right as I climb.

When I'm fairly certain I'm out of view of the windows on the front of the house, I start across the grassy area to the garage.

A dog barks. It sounds like it's coming from the house. Is anyone home?

More barking. It's not the yip of a small dog, but a big dog's deep and persistent woof. I stop and listen for a voice.

The front door creaks open. Someone *is* home. *Omigod! Someone is letting the dog out!*

I sprint back toward the woods. At first the dog just seems to be guarding lazily, barking its warning into the air. But then it hears me or picks up my scent and races after me. It's big and black and ferocious.

I scream at the top of my lungs and plow through tangled weeds into the trees. I turn up the hill toward a cluster of large boulders and scramble up one, hoping the dog won't be able to follow.

When I get to the top, I realize the dog is still barking—now more aggressively than ever—but it has stopped chasing me. It must be wearing an electric collar. I must have run out of its range.

Omigod.

I can hardly catch my breath. My heart tries to

pound its way out of my skin. Staying still feels too scary. I slide off the boulder and walk aimlessly away from the house.

I see a wide path, one likely made by farm equipment long ago and used by four-wheelers now. I'm tempted to follow it instead of trying to bushwhack my way back down to Old Post Road—and likely crossing another yard with dogs.

But who knows where this path comes out? Some of these old ones go on forever.

That's when I see something.

Something reflective.

Cautiously I pull back a large, low-hanging evergreen branch. There, tucked into the woods on the side of this path, is a car.

And the hood is seriously damaged.

Omigod! My instincts were correct. "I was right! I was right! I was right!" I say as I pull out my phone and snap multiple pictures.

I'm crouching, taking a picture of the license plate, when I hear, "It's true. You *were* right."

I jerk up.

It's Jax. He must have seen me running and followed.

He comes closer.

At this moment, it occurs to me that I'm looking at a kid who almost killed another kid. What might he do to me? But he looks more scared than dangerous.

"Oh, Jax. How could you do that?"

"It was me," he confesses, his voice trembling. "I hit Gray Olsen. But I didn't realize it right away. I'd been out clamming. I heard the thump when I hit him, but I thought it was a deer. Or a wild turkey. I didn't think anyone would be out walking on Winding Road at that hour."

I feel angry. I'm not sure if I'm angry on Gray's behalf or because Jax has put me in this position. The position of knowing the truth and having to decide what to do with it.

"But when you *did* realize you hit him, why didn't you go to the police?"

"I should have. I *know* I should have. But I kept thinking it was a bad dream and it would somehow all go away. But I'll do it now."

"What do you mean?"

"I'll turn myself in. I just . . . I need to wait until tomorrow."

"What? Why not now?"

"Mrs. Hobbs will be over tomorrow at noon to watch my grandfather. I promise I'll go as soon as she gets here." Then he adds, "They may go easier on me if I admit it."

At this moment, Jax doesn't look smirky or sneaky. He looks like a kid who's in a whole heap of trouble.

A kid who had an accident, a horrible moment that changed the course of Gray's life and his.

"How will I know you've actually done it?"

"Your mom's a reporter, right? Have her call the police station in the afternoon to confirm. If I haven't turned myself in, you can show them the photographs. You can tell them it was me, and they'll know where to find me."

It's easy to find the holes in this logic. His mother could easily whisk him off.

"You can trust me. I promise."

I think of that Shakespeare quote Bronwyn taught me: "Love all, trust a few . . ." But I don't want quotes in my head right now. I don't want someone else's wisdom.

I consider how easy it would be for him to take off running and hide somewhere, but I dismiss the idea. I can't explain why, but I do trust him. I decide to trust myself on this one.

"Okay," I say. "You have until two o'clock tomorrow."

He nods, visibly relieved. I'm not sure if it's because he has time or because he's no longer keeping this horrible secret.

I turn and start making my way back to the road.

"Hey!" he calls.

I look back.

"For what it's worth, I'd give anything to have been the one who called 911, to have been the one singing the song that brought him back. What you did was awesome."

"Thanks," I say, but my heart is tearing in two.

Chapter 33

Thank goodness I don't have to walk all the way back to Bluff's Head. As soon as I get to the intersection, Aunt Beth drives by.

She slows down and calls out through her open window, "That doesn't look like running to me."

Then she pulls over, and I spill into the passenger seat. "I overdid it my first time," I say as I buckle in. "I ran about two miles, though." (I figure running from a vicious dog multiplies my actual distance.)

"Not a bad start!" Aunt Beth says.

"I hope you wore sunscreen!" Grana says as I come in the door.

"I did," I say, hoping that my voice doesn't reveal the fact that I'm consumed with angsty feelings about Jax and what I now know for sure.

"Well, why don't you get a shower," she says, "and then we'll make strawberry pie. I picked without you."

Her words bounce right off me this afternoon.

I run the shower on the cool side, and it feels perfect. As water and peppermint shampoo run down my back, I think of Jax and his confession. I know that what he did was wrong; he shouldn't have been driving without a license, he should have investigated the thump, and he should have turned himself in to the police sooner. But still, he's just a kid who made a horrific mistake, and now he'll likely get juvenile detention. (Would he have gotten something worse if Gray had died? The thought makes me shudder.)

I step out of the shower and dry off. I need to tell Mom about Jax tonight so she can have the scoop on this story. This news flash, along with her article about people who confess to crimes they didn't commit, should land her a job at one of the big papers!

It occurs to me that she can't reveal Jax's name—he's a minor, and reporters can't provide the names of minors—and I feel oddly relieved about this. Folks will probably know soon enough that Mr. McCallister's grandson is the one who nearly killed Gray, but I'm glad it won't be my mom who discloses that.

Bronwyn is at play rehearsal, and Calla is with her folk group, so Dad drives just me to Mom's house after dinner.

"You were pretty quiet tonight," he says. "Everything okay?"

For some reason, his question makes me want to cry. I think of telling him what I discovered, but I feel disloyal telling him before Mom.

"Yeah," I say. "That run really wore me out. I don't know how Aunt Beth does nine miles."

"How far did you go?"

I don't want to lie more than I have to. "Up to Mr. McCallister's house. Do you know him?"

"I do," Dad says. "How do *you* know him?"

"I've seen him around town this summer. His grandson is staying with him."

"I remember when that boy was born," says Dad. "Will McCallister was the happiest grandfather alive."

I look at my dad, hoping he'll say more.

"He was the cook up at Brentwood when I was the boating instructor. I think he was there for more than thirty years. Made the best blueberry pancakes. Pretty sure it was because he cooked them up in bacon fat, though I've never been able to get the same flavor."

"So you know Jax, too?"

"Sure! Well, not now. But when he was younger, he attended camp. Loved being by the water."

He probably still does. I think of him taking care of his grandfather this summer instead of doing more of what he loves.

I'm dying to talk to Mom when I get home, but

she's on the phone. It sounds like it's with the guy she went on the date with. Her voice is irritatingly giggly.

So I start to prepare for bed. I change into pj's, wash my face, use my electric toothbrush for two whole minutes, and then start to brush my hair for one hundred strokes. But I get to stroke twenty-five and begin to question the need. Grana taught me the hundred-stroke technique, but I'm not sure it does my hair any good at all.

I toss the brush into the drawer and stretch out on top of my covers, waiting for Mom to get off the phone. My mind wanders back over this wild summer and everything that led to this moment—finding Gray, losing and gaining a job in the same day, holding Gray's hand as he woke up, almost losing my best friend, solving the mystery of the hit-and-run driver.

I think about the circumstances that led up to Jax hitting Gray, thinking he must wish he had never gone clamming, must wish he could take that moment back. There's something about this that almost conjures a thought, but my eyelids are heavy and the room is hot, so I fall into sleep instead.

Chapter 34

The next morning, even though I'm up before my sisters, Mom is already gone. *Darn it!* I write a quick note for Bronwyn and Calla, then grab my phone and water bottle. I snap on my helmet and head to the hospital. I'm a quarter mile down the road when I realize I forgot sunscreen. I consider going back but decide that I will probably live without it.

I hope I arrive at the hospital before Gray's other visitors. Perhaps he and I can have a late breakfast together. I imagine telling him just enough details of the hit-and-run to convince him that I'm worth knowing—worth *loving*, even—but not enough of the story that Mom is robbed again.

I remember reading in one of the magazines Mrs. Olsen bought me that guys like girls who are a little mysterious. I guess we'll see if it works!

The air is cooler this morning, and there's a slight breeze. It's refreshing.

I reach the section of Winding Lane where I found

Gray and can't help thinking about Jax. I wonder what he's doing right now.

How long ago the morning of the accident seems now. I was so eager to give Mari her card.

I recall the brightness. How the air felt cool and the water sparkled.

I stop pedaling and slow down.

Way down.

The water sparkled.

I remember that. I know it's true. I heard a boat and thought it might be Mari's father coming in early to take her to Gloucester.

The tide was high that morning.

That means Jax couldn't have been clamming.

Omigod.

He's lying.

Totally lying.

My first impulse is to ride directly to his house. But I don't.

He'll either be at the police station shortly after noon—which would be the safest place to confront him, since there will be no ferocious dog and nowhere for Jax to run—or he won't. If he isn't, I'll march directly into the station and tell them everything I know and let the professionals sort it all out.

This day feels momentous. I want to talk to my

parents. I want to talk to my sisters. But most of all, I want to talk to my best friend. When I get to the hospital, I park my bike and call Mari. I want to tell her everything.

She doesn't pick up.

I have to face facts. She's ignoring me.

When my call goes to voicemail, I leave a message. "I'm sorry if I've been a jerk," I say. "I want to make it right. I miss you."

I buy a blueberry muffin in the cafeteria and head up to Gray's room. Outside his door, Mrs. Olsen stands with a woman and a girl who's about my age. I recognize her immediately. She's the girl from the photograph. The one dressed up for the Spring Fling, standing next to Gray.

She is tall and smiley and wearing a pink sweat-shirt that says CUTE.

"Peyton," Mrs. Olsen says, sounding as pleased as always to see me. "Come meet Mrs. Michiko and Jordan. They arrived from Connecticut last night."

Jordan. Girl. Gray's best friend.

"You're the one who found Gray!" Jordan says. "And woke him up by singing that ridiculous song!"

I nod but don't say more. I'm sure they heard the story directly from Mrs. Olsen when it happened.

"It must have been awful to come across him in

the road," Jordan says. The way she says it makes me think she could be *my* best friend. I want to hate her, but I can't.

"Why don't you go in and see Gray," Mrs. Olsen says to Jordan and her mother, "and I'll sit out here with Peyton."

I feel the weight of her words. "Here," I say, handing the muffin to Jordan. "For Gray."

"His favorite," she says, and smiles. "Thanks." She follows her mother into his room.

"They've been friends since kindergarten," Mrs. Olsen says as she leads me to a sofa where we can sit down. "That's a long time for two kids to be thick as thieves, but there you have it. Jordan would do anything for Gray."

"And vice versa?" I ask. I don't know where the courage to ask comes from. But I can tell that Mrs. Olsen is protecting me, and I guess I don't want her to have to work so hard.

"I suppose so," she says, though I could swear from the look on her face that she has her doubts. And I wonder, does she question Gray's devotion to Jordan? Or does she question whether Gray is that devoted to anyone other than himself?

I try to banish the thought as soon as it enters my head. It's cruel and not something I should be thinking about someone who has suffered the way he has.

But the thought lingers. And I realize that in a strange way, it's sort of comforting not to feel pressure to focus only on the positive.

I so wanted him to be my boyfriend—my destiny. But I realize now that *destiny* sort of implies that you don't have to figure things out for yourself. It suggests the promise of not making a mistake . . . the same as my boyfriend list. If I've learned anything this summer, it's that the more I insist on things being the way they're supposed to be, the more I'm prevented from seeing (and accepting) things the way they really are.

Gray is not my first boyfriend.

I feel immediate relief when I admit this.

"I'm glad I have the chance to talk with you alone this morning, Peyton. I wanted to tell you in person that we're moving Gray back home in a day or two," she says gently.

"I guess that's good news, right?" I hope I sound convincing.

She takes one of my hands between hers and sighs. "I want you to know, Peyton, that I will be grateful to you for the rest of my life. You found my son, stopped, and called for help. You were someone to talk to during my darkest days. You stayed with Gray when I couldn't be here, and you sang him back to life. These are no small things for such a young woman."

Tears push at the back of my eyes. *These are no small things*, I think.

Then I realize: she's saying goodbye. And somehow I know she's saying it for herself and for Gray.

I expect to be swallowed by sadness. But I'm not. It's enough to know that I stepped up and played a part in saving a life.

"Thank you for giving me such an important first job," I say. "Obviously I'll never forget any of this."

"We'll stay in touch," Mrs. Olsen says, and stands.

It's time for me to go. "Please say goodbye to Gray for me."

I can tell by the relief on her face that she's glad I'm not insisting on doing it myself. But then her expression changes to one of sudden realization: "I haven't paid you!"

"It's not necessary," I tell her.

Mrs. Olsen shakes her head. "Nonsense, you should be compensated." She writes a check and hands it to me. "Thank you again, Peyton," she says.

When I get outside, the sun is bright. It takes time for my eyes to adjust. I have an hour and a half before meeting Jax at the police station. I could go home, but I decide to call Mom while treating myself to a donut at Day's.

I buy a raspberry jelly donut and sit on the bench

out front. I start to press call when I realize that although I have strong suspicions about what *really* happened and why Jax lied, I'm still speculating. After all, Jax could have clammed for a while and then slept out under the stars. Who knows? And if I've learned anything, it's that speculating can have unintended—and sometimes dire—consequences.

Just as I decide not to call Mom yet, my phone rings.

It's Mari.

I feel shaky as I accept the call.

"What's going on?" she says. I can tell that she's nervous, too.

"I'm so sorry, Mari. I've been such a rotten friend."

"What do you mean?" She sounds polite, like she hasn't been thinking the exact same thing for weeks.

"You can agree," I say. "I get it. I've been inconsiderate and too preoccupied with trying to control everything."

She's silent.

"In my life *and* yours," I say. "I'm going to cut it out, or at least try. No more quotes. And I want to hear about Jared."

"Okay," she says, sounding like my best friend again. "But first, tell me about Gray waking up!"

I tell her everything. I realize as we're talking that *she's* a really good listener. She doesn't interrupt, doesn't judge, doesn't try to tell me what's right or wrong.

I tell her that I'm going to try to be more like her.

"There you go again," she says.

"What?" I ask.

"Constantly trying to improve! You're a good person, Peyton. Trust yourself."

She's right about my constantly trying to improve, and I suddenly realize that it's been sort of exhausting. "I'll try," I say.

"Promise?" she asks.

It's funny how I thought being perfect would protect me from hurt and rejection, and then I nearly lost my best friend over it. "Promise," I say, though it will be a hard habit to break. "Now tell me all your juicy deets."

Mari and I are finally hanging up when I see Jax McCallister jogging into town. I jump up and grab my bike. But rather than going down Main Street, where I'm sitting, he cuts down a back alley, taking a more direct route to the police station.

I race to meet him and practically run him over.

"You lied to me," I say.

He's both confused and out of breath. "What are you talking about? I'm on my way, aren't I? Just like I said I would be!"

I position my bike to block his path. He glares at me.

"You weren't clamming on the day Gray was hit." I expect him to look defensive, maybe fearful, but his expression doesn't change. "It was high tide," I explain. "Not good for clamming."

"I must have been fishing that day, then. Anyway, what difference does it make?" He tries to move around my bike.

I grab his arm. "I think your whole story is a lie. Who was driving the car when it hit Gray?" I ask, working off my instincts.

"Me!" he says a little too forcefully. Then his lip begins to tremble. He pulls his arm free, then crouches low to the ground as if his stomach is seizing.

I jump off my bike and let it fall to the pavement. I reach out and touch his back to steady him.

"It was your grandfather, wasn't it?" I whisper.

He nods.

My hand suddenly feels awkward on his back. I slide it to my side.

He throws his head back and stares up at the sky. Then he turns to me. "My grandfather's sick," he says. "He doesn't know what he's doing."

"I know."

"My mom told me to hide the car keys, that he shouldn't be driving—and I did! But he found them before I woke up. When I realized he was gone, I figured he'd driven to Brentwood. Sometimes he still thinks he works there—that he has to get the coffee going for sleepy counselors. He gets pretty frantic when he thinks he's letting kids down."

Sadness rises to my throat.

"I hopped on Gramps's bike and raced over there. Sure enough, he was wandering right outside the kitchen, mumbling about the 'damn raccoons' and how so-and-so had forgotten to lock the trash house again. I finally got him back to the car. I tried to get the bike into the trunk, but it wouldn't fit—or maybe I was in too much of a hurry. I told my grandfather to stay put, and I raced to hide it on Winding Lane. When I got back to the car, my grandfather had buckled into the driver's seat.

"At this point, I wasn't really thinking well. I mean, I guess I thought that if my grandfather was able to drive himself to camp, he was able to drive us home. I should have known better. I should have called Mrs. Hobbs for help. I was just so relieved to find my grandfather. I guess I thought the crisis was over."

I cringe, knowing what's coming next.

"When my grandfather hit Gray Olsen, I was looking down at my phone. There was this large thump. 'Damn turkeys!' Gramps said, and I took his word for it. I didn't even bother to look back—I didn't want to see a turkey suffering in the road. It wasn't until we got home and I saw the damage that I realized it was probably something bigger. And even then, I thought he had likely hit a deer.

"That's when I hid the car in the woods. Not because I wanted to hide evidence, but because I didn't want to my grandfather to get behind the wheel ever again.

"When I heard about the hit-and-run on the news, I knew exactly what had happened. I know I should have gone straight to the police," he continues before I can say anything. "I should have told them what happened. But I couldn't stand the thought of my grandfather in jail! Not when it was my fault!"

"Jax," I say gently, resting a hand on his back again, "it's not your—"

He jumps up and begins pacing. "It was my job to watch him! I told my mom I could handle it, and I had been handling it! It was just that one mistake, that one time I didn't hide the keys well enough . . ." He turns away, and his shoulders begin to shake.

I stand and walk around so I can see his face. "Won't the police understand? Surely the law is different in situations like these." I have no idea if that's really true, but it should be!

Jax shrugs and shakes his head. "I've been trying to get him diagnosed," he says. "That's why we were at the hospital all those times. He was having a series of tests. So that if the truth came out, it would be really clear that my grandfather is not the type of man who leaves a kid to die. He's just not."

My mind is fuddled. What is right here, and what is wrong? Who is the guilty one? Who should be punished?

I have been so determined to see justice served, but I no longer know what justice looks like.

"I'm actually glad you found the car," he says, and starts walking toward the station. "This secret has been eating me alive."

I get my bike and walk beside him.

"You're not going to tell them that you were the one driving, are you?" I reach out and grab his hand to slow him down. "Your grandfather wouldn't want that, right?"

"I don't want my grandfather to know he almost killed a boy."

"Knowing you confessed to a crime he committed would be the very worst punishment of all for him."

Jax's face crumples. He nods knowingly.

Moments later, we're in front of the station.

"Okay. I'm doing it," he says. "I'm going in and telling the truth."

"Do you want me to come with you?"

He shakes his head.

"Here," he says, taking out his phone. "Give me

your number, and I'll text you as soon as I can."

We exchange numbers, and then I watch him walk into the police station.

More than anything, I want to talk to my mom right now. But I can't. Yes, I want her to be a big-time news reporter. Yes, I want her to break this story. But I can't tell her what I know. Not yet, anyway. It just doesn't feel right.

Bronwyn and Calla immediately stop talking when I enter the living room, clearly discussing something they don't want me to hear. No matter. I let them have their conversation and head into my room.

I think of texting Mari, but I'm too distracted.

I lie on my bed and look up at my wall—all those quotes telling me how to live my life. All those quotes promising me that if I just do the right thing, I will be happy. No more humiliation, like I experienced in the hospital room. No more gut-wrenching sadness, like the pain Jax is coping with.

I look up at one of them: "You can often change your circumstances by changing your attitude." That's Eleanor Roosevelt.

Yeah, maybe, I think. But sometimes you can't. Sometimes you can rise to the level of your best self, and sometimes you have to honor who you are in the moment. And maybe, just maybe, by letting go of who you think you should be, you become more of who you are meant to be.

Even though I know there's a lot of wisdom on this wall, I reach up and pull on the sticky tack that holds this particular handmade poster in place. It comes down easily.

So do the others.

I'm taking the last of the quotes off the wall when my phone dings.

Jax: Hey

Me: Hey! Are you OK?

Jax: Yeah. Officer Dorian was great. She's going to talk to the Olsens. We're hoping they won't press charges.

Me: Maybe I can talk to the Olsens, too? Mrs. Olsen might listen to me.

Jax: Maybe. Let's see what happens.

I know the Olsens have been as determined to find the driver as I have. I just hope they can be compassionate.

Jax: Mom's going to stay with Gramps and me until we can figure things out.

Me: What about her job?

Jax: She might lose it. She doesn't care. Can you meet me later?

Me: Sure. Just say when.

Moments later, Mom comes into my room.

"What's happening in here?" she asks. Now both sides of the room look like hurricane aftermath.

"I think I've outgrown these," I say, pointing to the quotes scattered all over my floor. "Don't worry: I'll clean them up."

Mom sits down next to me on the bed.

"You want to talk about it?"

I sigh. "I can't believe that just two weeks ago, I was certain of so many things."

"It's a trap we all fall into," Mom says. "I still do on a regular basis. The one quote I try hard to remember is, 'The only constant in life is change.'"

"Thanks, but I'm kind of done with quotes right now."

She ruffles my hair. "Thought you might like to know that the editor at *BDN* called me today."

I sit up tall. "And?"

"He offered me a regular beat."

I bounce. "Seriously?"

"I turned him down," Mom says.

I look at her wide-eyed. She's wanted this for so long.

"All this time, I've been chasing the hard-hitting news stories because I thought I'd finally be taken seriously. It turns out that what I really want is something slightly different. I want to cover the stories that

I wish *others* would take seriously—and I can do that best as a freelancer."

This day has been so topsy-turvy. "What sorts of stories?"

"Well, to begin with, I think I'll write a story on Alzheimer's and how hard it can be on other family members."

Oh.

I take a deep breath. "Like Mr. McCallister's family?"

She searches my eyes.

"I know," I say. "I know it was him. I decided that I didn't feel right being the one who shared that news. I'm sorry I didn't tell you."

"I understand," she says. "And I'm proud of you for honoring the family's need for privacy. I learned this afternoon and decided to do the same."

I feel equally proud of my mom. (And a little proud of the fact that I'm like her.) "The right thing is not always as obvious as I thought it would be."

"Exactly," she says.

I should have known that Mom wouldn't jump to reveal Mr. McCallister's guilt. It's not that she isn't persistent. It's not that she gives up easily. (How could I have thought that?) It's that she considers things from many different angles. Like the way she protected me by not writing that human-interest story. She could have been the one to report on her daughter finding Gray, her daughter singing "Try, Try, Try" and bringing him out of the coma. But she made the decision she thought was best for everyone.

I'm popping out of my skin by the time Jax texts again. We're already having supper. Mom agrees to let me ride to the town dock as long as I'm home before dark. I figure I can spend one hour with him.

He's sitting on a bench when I arrive but stands and walks toward me as I approach. "Sorry I didn't text you sooner," he says. "I had to watch my grandfather while my mother made a gazillion calls. He can't stay in his house any longer."

That's so sad, I think as we make our way back to the bench.

"But I have some good news," he adds. "The Olsens are not going to press charges. I got the sense that it was more Mrs. Olsen's doing than Mr. Olsen's."

I feel a huge sense of relief and a sudden flood of happiness in the place where fear had settled. "Was your mom calling nursing homes?"

He nods. I can tell the thought makes him sad.

"Will he mind?" I ask.

"Undoubtedly. It's so hard to be the ones telling him what to do. He was the best grandfather. I spent every summer with him at camp. On his hours off, he'd teach a group of us how to fish, or clam, or throw baseballs." He grins. "Sometimes we'd clean the fish and cook them over the campfire. I'm not the only one with fond memories of him. I was so proud that he was my granddad."

"My mom knows it was your grandfather," I say quietly. "I didn't say anything to her—promise—but she found out somehow. Maybe through her contact at the police station. She doesn't want to write about it, though. She wants to respect what your family is going through."

"Seems like you and your mom are close."

I feel the old resistance rising up in me, the fear that I will be unlovable if I'm too much like her, but then I think of the brave decisions she's made. It couldn't have been easy living with my grandmother, especially when my father didn't stick up for my mom the way he did for me the other day. And Dad didn't really support her; I see that now. He didn't even go to Grandpa's funeral. Maybe he was never there when she needed him.

I'm filled with truth. Mom is not unlovable. She just wasn't with the right person. And while the formula for choosing the right one isn't as simple as I thought, it was never my mom who needed fixing. Maybe I don't need fixing, either.

"Hey," Jax says. "Give me your phone." His voice is lighter. He's back to his playful self.

"Why?" I ask, but I give it to him just the same.

"Move in closer to me."

I momentarily glance at the sky, knowing I have to judge when it'll be dark.

He snaps a picture of us both looking up. It's sort of funny.

"Now," he says, scrolling through my contacts, "who's your best friend?"

"Why? What are you doing?"

"I want to say hello. And send her this picture."

"What?" I grab for my phone. He doesn't give it up.

"I won't flirt. I figured I could check off numbers nine and five at the same time."

Omigod.

Omigod! Number nine: *Take funny pictures together.* Number five: *Talk (but not flirt) with my best friend.*

"You lied! You told me you didn't read my list!"

He gives me a sheepish grin. "I didn't want to embarrass you."

"That list is ridiculous," I say. "I'm going to tear it up!"

"No, don't. Next time we see each other, give it back to me if you don't want it."

"Why?" My thoughts keep tumbling over the words *next time*.

"Because," he says. "You wrote it. And it makes me smile."

I take my time riding home, looking out at the still water reflecting pinks and oranges from the sun setting on the other side of the peninsula.

When I arrive, I see that I have another text.

Jax: Don't forget to send that selfie to Mari

I feel a rush of joy from my head to the tips of my toes.

Me: Yeah, yeah
Jax: Oh, and Peyton?
Me: Yeah?
Jax: I know it's crossed off, so maybe it
doesn't count, but I just wanted you to
know . . .
Me: Yeah???
Jax: I really love Narnia.

I smile and slide my phone back into my pocket. I have no idea what tomorrow will hold, let alone anything beyond that . . .

And I can't wait.